"I se... ... ... the wrong things to you."

Angus spoke gently, turning her face toward him. "I don't mean to, Sarah."

Sarah stared helplessly into his eyes. She was a country girl, homespun and honest. She had never learned to deceive anyone.

She loved Angus. How simple it would be to tell him of her feelings, but she knew she never could. Angus Sawyer didn't believe in love and marriage. She did!

"What is it, Sarah?" he asked softly when she didn't answer. She shook her head, the lump in her throat preventing speech. He sighed. "Whenever I think I'm getting closer to you, you suddenly blot me out, slam the door in my face." He dragged a hand through his hair. "Do you really dislike me so much?"

If only he knew!

Rosemary Badger, an Australian author, says she always wanted to write, but only started seriously after she took a creative writing course on how to create books specifically for the romance market. Her novels are usually set in Australia, which she knows so well. The author is married and lives with her husband and children in Queensland.

Books by Rosemary Badger

HARLEQUIN ROMANCE

Don't miss any of our special offers. Write to us at the following address for information on our newest releases.

Harlequin Reader Service
901 Fuhrmann Blvd., P.O. Box 1397, Buffalo, NY 14240
Canadian address: P.O. Box 603,
Fort Erie, Ont. L2A 5X3

The Good-Time Guy

Rosemary Badger

Harlequin Books

TORONTO • NEW YORK • LONDON
AMSTERDAM • PARIS • SYDNEY • HAMBURG
STOCKHOLM • ATHENS • TOKYO • MILAN

Original hardcover edition published in 1987
by Mills & Boon Limited

ISBN 0-373-02864-4

Harlequin Romance first edition October 1987

For Tara-Lee and Trevor

Copyright © 1987 by Rosemary Badger.
Philippine copyright 1987. Australian copyright 1987.
All rights reserved. Except for use in any review, the reproduction or utilization
of this work in whole or in part in any form by any electronic, mechanical
or other means, now known or hereafter invented, including xerography,
photocopying and recording, or in any information storage or retrieval system,
is forbidden without the permission of the publisher, Harlequin Enterprises
Limited, 225 Duncan Mill Road, Don Mills, Ontario, Canada M3B 3K9. All the
characters in this book have no existence outside the imagination of the
author and have no relation whatsoever to anyone bearing the same name
or names. They are not even distantly inspired by any individual known
or unknown to the author, and all incidents are pure invention.

The Harlequin trademarks, consisting of the words HARLEQUIN ROMANCE
and the portrayal of a Harlequin, are trademarks of Harlequin Enterprises
Limited; the portrayal of a Harlequin is registered in the United States Patent
and Trademark Office and in the Canada Trade Marks Office.

Printed in U.S.A.

CHAPTER ONE

'REALLY, Miss...'

'Ames,' Sarah supplied quickly, her chestnut-coloured hair swirling in soft waves across her shoulders as she leaned forward in her chair, her beautiful green eyes desperate as she pleaded with the receptionist. 'Please,' she begged, 'couldn't you at least test me for the job? I can do it, I know I can, if only you would...'

'I've already explained to you, Miss Ames,' the receptionist cut in impatiently, 'the agency sent you by mistake. You're only, what? She picked up the blue card with Sarah's rather remarkable credentials and scanned it briefly. 'Ah, yes, twenty-one. Far too young for the job and with only part-time experience. We need someone *much* older. In short, Miss Ames, we need a highly qualified professional person. We don't need a fresh young girl who *thinks* she knows everything just because she graduated from Business College!'

Sarah picked up her blue card and tucked it into her handbag. She stood up, green eyes sparkling with a defiance borne out of the frustration several days of job-hunting had given her. 'I demand to see the manager!' she declared stiffly. 'I'm fully qualified for this job and have a right to be properly interviewed.'

'You will leave this office this *instant*!' the blonde receptionist snapped. She stood up briskly, thin eyebrows raised imperiously over cold blue eyes, daring Sarah to question her authority.

Sarah straightened her shoulders. 'I will leave,' she answered softly, '*after* I've been interviewed.'

The receptionist gasped at this outrageous display of disobedience. How dare this young thing speak to *her* like that!

'Problems, Kirsten?' a deep voice enquired.

Sarah's head swung around to face the owner of that voice. A tall man, well over six feet, was lounging comfortably against the door and, judging from the amused mockery in his black eyes he had been listening to the conversation between Sarah and the receptionist.

He pinned Sarah with his gaze, heavily lashed eyes seemingly committing to memory every feature and bringing a deep flush to her cheeks. He was handsome, ruggedly so, thick black hair brushed back from a wide intelligent brow. His mouth was full, sensuous, hinting at a raw sexuality, below a straight, long nose, the nostrils slightly flared. Wide powerful shoulders tapered down to a narrow waist and lean hips. Light grey trousers hugged muscular thighs while the crisp whiteness of his shirt enhanced the deep brown tan of his skin. His suit-jacket was flung casually over one shoulder.

He was extremely handsome by anyone's standards, and a pleasant change from the rather paunchy businessmen Sarah had come across during her exercise of job-hunting. He was also obviously a man in authority, his confidence and assurance making him seem much older than he appeared, as Sarah judged him to be somewhere in his early thirties.

She bit her lip in confusion as he continued to stare at her, not realising that wild horses couldn't have dragged her own eyes away; that her scrutiny of him was every bit as intense as his was of her!

The receptionist, Kirsten, broke the spell. 'Problems, indeed!' she snapped, circling her desk to stand next to Sarah while the man pushed himself away from the door and walked with long strides towards them. 'This . . . this *child* was sent to us by one of the agencies we go through. *By mistake*, I might add, and even though I've explained why we can't use her she has insisted that she be interviewed.'

The man smiled at Sarah, a strangely intimate smile which brought a warm flush to her smooth cheeks. 'Why can't we use her?' he asked, his black eyes resting on Sarah's green ones. He must be the manager, Sarah was thinking, hope replacing despair as she dared to think she might, just might, land a job at Sawyer Electronics, Queensland's largest exporting firm of electronic equipment with their head office based here in Brisbane.

She returned the man's smile, encouraging him to agree that she should at least be granted an interview, a chance to prove that she was capable of the job. His black eyes narrowed on that smile, his own disappearing.

'Because she's too young, for one thing,' the receptionist explained, her tone losing the self-assuredness she had displayed earlier. 'And she's had no previous experience. She couldn't possibly handle the job.'

'And what job are we discussing?' he asked, turning those incredibly black eyes on to the receptionist.

'Office manager for our new plant,' Kirsten laughed, obviously thinking the man would also, at how ridiculous this whole thing was. 'She's only twenty-one and expects to start at the top, like the majority of her peers,' she added sarcastically, frowning suddenly because the man *wasn't* laughing.

'Initiative is something to be admired, Kirsten,' he drawled softly. 'It surprises me that you should consider it amusing.' He turned back to Sarah. 'Come into my office.'

If the reception area to this vast and wealthy establishment was magnificent with its blue and gold furnishings, then this man's office was truly superb. The room was huge, one wall entirely of glass, offering panoramic views of the bustling city below, while the Brisbane river wound its way like a thin blue ribbon through the maze of modern office towers. Another wall housed leather-bound volumes of books, while expensive prints and original oil paintings filled another. The beige carpeting was thick and luxurious, the furniture in burgundy-red leather. Soft lighting gave an intimately warm feeling, helped along by teak-panelled walls and a well-stocked bar.

Sarah stood just inside the door, tall and slender, her hair appearing almost auburn under the soft glow of the lights. His dark gaze flicked over her, from the shining waves which hugged her slender neck down to the smart two-piece brown business-suit which outlined the perfection of her body and showed off long legs thrust into neat high heels. His eyes returned to her face, a perfect heart shape, the hair flowing from its centre parting, the clear green eyes surrounded by silky dark lashes, the small pert nose and the slightly pouting mouth.

Sarah felt him watching her, could feel the warmth of those black eyes as she looked slowly around the office, a feeling of apprehension hitting her stomach as it suddenly dawned on her who this man was. He was no manager! He was, had to be, Angus Sawyer himself! And she had heard enough stories about Angus Sawyer to make her want to turn and flee. Rich and powerful, he had made his way to the top by cutting down anyone who got in his way. He was ruthless, domineering, a brilliant businessman— but he was also a womaniser with an insatiable appetite which had left a trail of broken hearts in his wake. Oh, yes, she had heard about his exploits during her two years in Brisbane, had read about him in newspapers and magazines, and she had even seen him interviewed on television.

She had thought him handsome in a harsh sort of way, had even smiled at some of his outrageously arrogant statements while he was being interviewed, but nothing had prepared her for the Angus Sawyer in the flesh! She had felt his animal magnetism from the second she had laid eyes on him, had been inexorably drawn to him, and if that wasn't bad enough, she had smiled at him, had blatantly encouraged him! At least that's what he must have thought she had done. No wonder he had invited her into his office. He probably thought she was on the make, that she had used the excuse of demanding to be interviewed as a ploy to meet him.

Her cheeks were flushed as she turned to look up at him, green eyes challenging. 'You . . . must be Mr Sawyer,' she said in a surprisingly calm voice. 'You're not . . . the manager.'

'Heavens, no!' He raised black brows in mock horror.

'I was to see the manager,' she answered stiffly.

'Won't I do?' he queried softly, voice taunting.

His voice intrigued her as it had when she had heard him being interviewed. It was husky, seductive, a bedroom voice! And she wasn't going to be intimidated by it, or swept in by his practised charms.

'You must be so busy,' she parried with a dismissive shrug of her shoulders.

'Not too busy to interview a beautiful young woman who wants to work for me,' he answered suggestively, deep grooves appearing attractively in his hard cheeks. This man had it all ... even dimples! Sarah turned away from him, the only way she could think of to safeguard herself against his charms. She felt his hand on her arm, the touch undeniably pleasant as he led her across the room to one of the leather-bound chairs facing his impressive desk. She would have shrugged discreetly from his grip but decided it would be better to have him think his touch did absolutely nothing to her.

'Thank you,' she murmured politely, her head barely reaching his shoulder, before she sat on the chair he offered, her arm feeling suddenly cold when he removed his hand.

'Well, Miss Ames,' he said, after having taken his place behind the desk and gazing across at her. Her cheeks flushed.

By his use of her name she knew he *had* listened to her conversation with his receptionist and that she had practically *begged* for this interview. 'So you want a job. And not just *any* job. You want to be my new office manager!' He made it sound rather amusing.

She met his gaze unflinchingly, her chestnut-coloured hair falling over one shoulder. 'Yes,' she replied firmly, chin lifted. 'I graduated with honours from the business college I attended.' She reached into her handbag and passed him the blue card which proved she had. He held the card in his huge tanned hands, studying it carefully, while Sarah pretended a lack of interest by concentrating on the suit-jacket he had tossed on to the desk.

'Most impressive,' he drawled, handing her back the card. 'But theory can sometimes be difficult when put into practice.'

'I've had practical experience, Mr Sawyer,' she quickly answered, tucking the card into her handbag. 'At the college ...'

'At the college you worked under tutorship,' he broke in. 'You're expected to make mistakes. In *my* business, there's no room for error: that's why I insist on hiring experienced personnel. Their teething problems are well and truly behind them by the time they get to me.'

Arrogant swine, she thought. Aloud she said, 'But you ... you said you admired ... initiative.'

'And indeed I do. Not many people would dare to stand up to my receptionist the way you did!' He chuckled. 'But I can see you're disappointed about the job.' He leaned back in his chair, hands clasped behind his head as he peered at her through hooded lids. 'You're too good to lose, far too beautiful and intelligent to pass over to an employer who might not appreciate you. I've already decided on an office manager, but she will need an assistant.' His smile was charming, roguishly so. 'How would you like to be my new *assistant* office manager?' And he named a salary which took her breath away. She hadn't expected to earn anything near that for several years.

'Well, what do you say?' he asked when she made no reply. 'Do you want the job or don't you?'

'I ... I need to think,' she answered. It was obvious he had created the job just for her, but what did he expect in return? His reputation with women couldn't be ignored but his offices were here while the new plant where she would be working was on the other side of town. He would probably pop in from time to time, but it was highly unlikely that she would see much of him.

And then there was the salary. She would be able to send money home, help her mother out with the younger children. Her brother, Billy, was clever and he would soon be graduating from high school. He deserved a chance at university. She would be able to help him. Her mind raced on, aware that Mr Sawyer was watching her, waiting for her answer, but still she hesitated. She wasn't used to men like him, being from a small country town in Queensland's outback where the men were *nice*! Quiet, maybe even dull, but nice. They would never take advantage of an innocent girl—and she was innocent.

During her two years in Brisbane she had hardly dated. Holidays saw her at home helping out on the farm on which years of drought and hardship had killed her father, leaving her mother to raise a family with next to no income. She would never have had the opportunity to study in Brisbane and earn a decent wage if it hadn't been for the scholarship she had won, and which her mother had insisted she accept. And now here she was, hesitating over a job which promised great rewards because she was afraid of the man who offered it! Afraid of his charm, his handsome good looks, but most of all afraid of the way he looked at her which made her blood run hot. He was dangerous and she knew it but for the sake of her family she knew what her answer must be. She cleared her throat and ran the tip of her tongue over dry lips.

'Your offer is very generous, Mr Sawyer,' she answered hesitantly. 'I accept and . . . and thank you.'

He regarded her thoughtfully through narrowed eyes. 'For someone who was so eager to work here you don't seem over-pleased now that you have the job,' he drawled. 'What's wrong? Salary not up to your expectations?'

'Oh, no,' she answered quickly. 'The salary is fine, really, it's just that . . .' Her voice trailed off. How could she tell him she never expected to be working directly for the great man himself, that she had assumed he was merely a figurehead in this wealthy establishment, perched high in his tower, while the little people did the work.

'Yes?' he prompted, leaning forward now in his chair, muscular arms folded across the desk, black eyes keenly watching her, studying the emotions which danced freely across her beautiful features. 'You're wondering now if you might have strayed beyond your depths, hm? Perhaps you're even afraid of me, is that it?' he taunted softly.

She looked at him unflinchingly. 'I'm not afraid of you, Mr Sawyer, nor do I doubt I can handle the job. I was just ... wondering if you really needed an assistant manager.'

'I don't really need anything,' he chuckled softly, 'so it's up to you to prove me wrong.' His black eyes hardened. 'You will be on a three-months' trial, and during that time I think you will find I'm a firm but fair boss. I don't tolerate absenteeism and I expect all my employees to earn every cent of their wage.'

'Of course; I didn't mean ...' She floundered badly, unnerved by his tone.

'Don't feel I'm doing you any favours by giving you this job, Miss Ames,' he continued as if she hadn't spoken. 'I'm running a business, not a benevolent society!'

Her green eyes sparkled angrily. 'I'll remember, Mr Sawyer. I appreciate your professionalism concerning your employees.'

Black eyes narrowed shrewdly. 'Good!'

'Yes, I'm relieved to know you don't grant favours and I think it's important for you to understand that I am the same. *I* don't grant favours either!'

His mouth twitched. 'Meaning?' he drawled

in that suggestive tone which was beginning to
grate on her nerves. He got up and stood in front
of her, leaning against his desk, long legs
stretched in front of him, the fabric of his grey
slacks stretching dangerously over his taut
muscular thighs. Sarah's cheeks flushed a deep
crimson as she quickly turned away, disgusted
that he should so openly flaunt his masculinity
and angry with herself that she should be so
affected by it! This man, this conceited, arrogant
man was deliberately trying to seduce her, she
felt sure of it. But he was also the man who had
given her a job with a fantastic salary which
could do so much for her family. Remembering
this, Sarah bit back the sharp retort which
hovered on her lips and forced herself to look up
at him, her smile tight as she said, 'Meaning I
understand about the three-months' trial and
that there's to be no absenteeism, nor are you
running a benevolent society.'

He grinned, deep grooves appearing attractively in his handsome face. 'You left out about
me being a firm but fair boss.'

She would have had to be made of stone to
resist the power of that smile, and she wasn't
made of stone! The corners of her mouth lifted
and she answered softly, 'I thought that went
without saying. That and the fact you expect
your employees to earn every cent of their wage,'
she finished breathlessly, still drawn in by his
smile, teeth dazzling white against his tanned
skin.

He reached for her hand and pulled her to her feet, his thighs brushing against hers as he held her against him, the tips of her breasts pressing against the hard wall of his chest before she stepped awkwardly back, only to feel the chair against her legs. His smile broadened at her dilemma, and she snatched her hand away, green eyes glaring up at him.

'I trust the interview is over?' she snapped, side-stepping away and reaching for her handbag.

'Apparently it is,' he drawled, watching while she tucked her bag under her arm in preparation for leaving. 'And I must say this is one interview I've enjoyed,' he added softly, seductively, black eyes lingering on her mouth.

Sarah straightened, refusing to notice his all-too-obvious interest in her; an interest which was blatantly sexual and came under the heading of 'sexual harassment'. They had been warned about this at the college, had been told how to handle it, but as she gazed helplessly up at him she realised the lessons hadn't included dealing with the lethal charms of the devil!

'When do I start my job, Mr Sawyer?' she asked.

'Monday,' he informed her. 'Do you know where it is?'

'Yes. What time Monday?'

'Your hours will be nine to five and you will be required to work on the occasional Saturday morning. Will that interfere with your love-life?'

She blinked up at him, frowning. 'Whatever do you mean?'

'Your date will have to get you home early on the Friday night so that you can cope with the job Saturday morning. I expect my employees to be wide awake and fully alert when they report for work.'

'I'm sure you do, Mr Sawyer,' she murmured, wondering if the same rule applied to himself. 'But you needn't worry about me. I haven't the time for dates.'

Black brows rose mockingly. 'Is that so?'

It was obvious he didn't believe her, and this rankled. 'Yes, that's so! Not all of us are bent on having a good time; some of us like to put our time to good use.'

Jet-black eyes glittered with amusement. 'And of course you're one of them! Tell me, Miss Ames, how *do* you spend your spare time?'

'I study,' she answered simply, not caring if he considered her dull. 'At the university, three nights a week. Accounting.' There, she thought smugly, enjoying the look of surprise which flashed in his eyes. Now he'll know I have no time for any nonsense!

'What do you do on the other four nights?' he asked casually, hooking his thumbs into the waistband of his trousers. He removed one large hand and held it up, stopping her as she was about to answer. 'No, let me guess. You work on assignments, pore over notes, right?'

'Right,' she answered firmly, nodding her

shining chestnut head to confirm that this was so.

His eyes rested on her face for several nerve-racking seconds before he turned abruptly away, circling his desk and sitting behind it in the huge executive-type chair.

'I believe you were leaving, Miss Ames,' he drawled, and she flushed at the rude manner in which she was being suddenly dismissed.

'Yes,' she curtly agreed, turning swiftly and walking across the vast expanse of luxurious broadloom. At the door his voice halted her.

'*Miss Ames!*'

Sarah swung around, certain he was going to withdraw the offer of her job, that she had angered him, that he had decided after all that he really didn't need an assistant manager at the plant, that he didn't need *her*! She swallowed hard, eyes filled with dark apprehension as she faced him across the room. 'Yes?' She was barely able to whisper, her voice sounding hoarse.

'Now that you are one of my employees I shall be calling you by your first name. Sarah.' He drawled out her name making it sound somehow beautiful, not plain like she considered it to be. 'And my name is Angus. You can call me that if you like.'

She shook her head. 'No, thank you. I wouldn't feel comfortable calling my boss by his first name,' she answered honestly. She smiled suddenly, her beautiful features lighting up. 'But thank you just the same.'

Out on the busy street Sarah turned and gazed

up at Sawyer Electronics just as she had done over an hour ago. But this time when she looked at the modern glass tower block she had a feeling of elation instead of despair. She had stepped out of the ranks of the unemployed and had won herself a job. And not just any old job either, she couldn't help but applaud herself. She had a title and a salary which did it justice. She, Sarah Ames, was an Assistant Office Manager!

She rang her mother from the pay-phone down the corridor from her room, which she was still lucky enough to have at the college during the summer break. Her mother was full of praise about her new job, as was her younger sister.

'How is everything, Mom?' Sarah finally asked. 'And I haven't spoken to Billy yet. Isn't he home?'

'Billy's helping Mr Porter with his hay crop,' her mother answered, 'and, yes, everything's fine here. I don't want you worrying about us; you've got your job to think about now.'

Sarah smiled. Her mother was determined that her children should get their chance in life and not be held back by family problems.

'Mom,' Sarah said softly into the mouthpiece, 'I'm an adult now, remember? I know everything isn't fine. Is Billy getting paid for helping with the hay crop?'

'Mr Porter will give him something when it's all finished. He usually does.'

Sarah frowned. Mr Porter was a wealthy man but mean when it came to paying for services received. Billy would be lucky to get anything at all, let alone what he was worth! Mr Porter liked to think people helped him out of the goodness of their hearts.

'What about Nellie, Mom?' Sarah changed the subject, not wanting to get into a discussion about Mr Porter whom her mother would only end up defending. 'Will the dentist be able to fix her teeth?' Nellie had broken her two top front teeth during a field hockey game and needed to have them capped.

'I haven't got around to taking her yet, dear,' her mother sighed. 'Things have been so hectic lately.'

Sarah chewed on her bottom lip. There just wasn't the money for Nellie's teeth and she knew it. Her fifteen-year-old sister would hate smiling with half of her two front teeth missing! Thank heavens for her wonderful, wonderful job. She would see that Nellie got her caps.

'Tell Nellie to hold on for just a bit longer, Mom. I'll be able to send money home on a regular basis now.'

'That will be wonderful, dear, but I think you'll find there will be precious little left once you pay for rent and food and all those other bills which come in on a regular basis.'

Sarah felt homesick after speaking to her family. Her mother was right. She was paying a nominal fee for her room at the college and received two meals a day for a basic amount, but once she found a flat, which she must do now that she had a job, her living expenses would increase dramatically.

But she was too full of hope to be homesick for long, and the more she thought of her job the more excited she became. She looked for a flat and found one half-way between the university and her job. It was in a fairly new building, was bright, airy and clean and had two bedrooms. Her mother or one of the children might come and stay with her for a bit. The flat was partially furnished, having two single beds, a small two-seater sofa, a coffee-table, two end-tables with lamps, a table and two chairs in the kitchen. Certainly enough to start out with, and she was enormously proud of her new little home.

On Sunday she decided she would take a bus to the plant, and familiarise herself with the route and the new surroundings. The plant was a five-minute walk from the bus stop and situated in beautifully landscaped gardens with newly planted shrubs and trees. The building was long and low, white, with large windows. In front of the impressively modern building was a large sign which bore the words *Sawyer Electronics— Factory Sales*. Sarah stood looking at the sign for several minutes, her face animated with delight.

She wished she could get inside, have a good look around, but of course the place was locked and probably equipped with all sorts of sophisticated electronic burglar alarms. Still, it wouldn't do any harm to have a peek through the windows, perhaps even see where her office was located and what it looked like.

Rolling up the sleeves of her green cotton shirt tucked into the band of her jeans, Sarah walked cautiously across the newly laid turf in her sandshoes. She peered in the front windows first, the reception area obviously, with its tastefully decorated rooms of pale green and beige and soft plush chairs and couches. There were several offices, each a little different but all extremely functional with up-to-the-minute office equipment, all electronically Sawyer of course! She wondered which office would be hers.

Slowly she worked her way around, coming at last to the back of the long building. A noise coming from within stopped her. She stood still but when she heard nothing more decided it must have been her imagination. At the very end of the building she came across large warehouse doors. One of them was raised. She heard movement inside, the unmistakable sound of furniture being shifted. Sarah stepped cautiously inside, unable to resist the temptation of seeing what her first real place of employment looked like.

This was the storage area, with huge crates and boxes. Next she came across a large assembly section, row upon row of work-tables and benches. A door banged and her heart leapt to her throat. For the first time she realised what a risk she had taken entering the building. She turned immediately, silently retracing her steps. The storage area was dark now with the roller doors closed. She could barely see where she was going, making her way more by memory than by sight.

Strong hands reached out and grabbed her, pinning her arms behind her and shoving her roughly against one of the wooden crates. A terrified scream died in her throat as she stared up at a giant of a figure, his body and face in almost total darkness. Only his eyes could be seen. The black eyes of the devil gleaming menacingly down at her! Sarah did what any normal young girl would do in a similar situation.

She fainted!

CHAPTER TWO

'You idiot! I should thrash you!'

Sarah blinked up at Angus Sawyer. She was stretched out on a couch with an ice-pack on her head, her cheeks pale.

'I ... I must have fainted,' she said weakly, trying to sit up, only to be pushed none too gently back on to the cushions propped behind her. She attempted a smile. 'I ... I thought you were a burglar!'

'What the hell did you think I thought *you* were?' he rasped angrily, grabbing the ice-pack and feeling the bump on the back of her head, his hands surprisingly gentle compared to his voice. He stood up and glared down at her, his face almost as black as the sweatshirt he was wearing, his stance menacing, jean-clad legs spread slightly apart, hands held in fists at his sides. 'You're damned lucky to be alive!'

Her eyes widened. 'You wouldn't have shot me!' She wetted her lips, her expression wary. 'Would you have?' she asked suspiciously.

'You deserved to be shot! What are you doing here? Snooping?'

Her cheeks blazed with colour. 'Certainly not! What a terrible thing to suggest.'

'What a terrible thing to *do*!' He reached down

27

and picked up the ice-pack, tossing it on to a window-bench of the well-equipped infirmary. Angus Sawyer's employees only received the best, she was beginning to realise. 'Well?' he growled. 'What excuse do you have for prowling around my plant?'

She shifted into a sitting position. 'I suppose I do owe you an explanation,' she began, only to have him bellow,

'You're damned right you do, and it had better be good!'

'Well, if you stop shouting for a moment and give me a chance . . .'

'Shouting?' he roared. 'God, woman, do you know what you've done? What the consequences could have been? When you have several million dollars' worth of equipment in a place like this you don't stand around asking questions when you think you're being burglarised!'

'But it was only *me*! A woman! Surely you didn't feel threatened by a mere woman?' she bit out, unable to hold back her sarcasm in the face of his rage.

'With you dressed the way you are and with that plait down your back, I mistook you for a man. It was only when I felt your . . .' His sudden smile told her only too well what it was he had felt! The smile disappeared as quickly as it had appeared, the black rage returning. 'Well? What are you waiting for? What excuse do you have for being here?' He leaned against the window-bench, arms folded across his chest, thick black hair falling over his brow as he waited for her answer.

Sarah shrugged. 'I wanted to see what the place looked like,' she stated simply.

He stared at her. 'You wanted to see what the place looked like?' he repeated disbelievingly. 'You couldn't wait until tomorrow?'

'Of course I could have waited, but I wanted to have a trial run on the bus, see how long it took from my place and how far I had to walk from the bus stop to here. I *like* being organised, Mr Sawyer,' she added with a sigh, her silky dark lashes shading the cool green of her eyes.

'Are you all right?' he enquired quickly as she pressed a slender hand to her head. He knelt beside her, smoothing back the coils of hair which had escaped from her plait, tucking them behind shell-like ears.

'What did you hit me with?' she groaned. 'A crowbar?'

'I didn't hit you with anything,' he said with exasperation.

'No? Then why do I have this big bump on the back of my head?'

'It's not a big bump.' He felt it. 'It's practically gone. You banged your head against one of the crates when I grabbed you.'

'Grabbed *and* pushed me,' she pointed out. 'Did you *really* think I was a burglar?' she asked, a mischievous twinkle in her eyes as she looked into his own which were strangely intent.

'I don't think it's a laughing matter!' he

ground out, standing suddenly, his whole body taut, rigid.

Sarah frowned. 'I wasn't laughing.' She laughed. 'For goodness sake, can't we forget about this? It's over and done with, and apart from this bump on my head no harm has been done.'

'Perhaps more harm than you realise,' he said in a husky voice, eyes narrowed.

Sarah stiffened. For the first time she sensed real danger. She swallowed hard. 'But you said ... you said I'm going to be fine, that the bump is small, practically gone.' She ran the tip of her tongue over dry lips, the gesture provocative in its innocence. Why was he looking at her like that?

'You will be fine,' he said. 'You shouldn't have come here today. It was a mistake, a *big* mistake!'

'I said I was sorry.' Her voice was a murmur.

'I didn't mean that!' He swept a hand through his hair. 'And you didn't say you were sorry.'

'But I am.' She swung her long legs off the couch and rose shakily to her feet. He grabbed her elbow, supporting her, his fingers digging into her soft flesh, hurting her. She looked pointedly down at his hand. 'I can manage on my own, thank you.' He smiled and dropped his hand. She looked around the room, feeling trapped, wanting to leave but lacking the courage to go. It was as if she were being held by a strange, invisible force. That was ridiculous. There was nothing here, just herself and ... *him*!

But he wasn't keeping her here. He wasn't even touching her. It had to be the bump on her head, and she reached up to feel for it, to reassure herself that it was still there, affecting her in some strange way. She might be suffering from concussion.

She turned to face him, forcing herself to take deep even breaths, her breasts gently heaving under the green cotton shirt. 'You're very beautiful,' he said softly, touching her flushed cheek with the back of his hand.

She pushed his hand away, stepping well away from him, her head held back, green eyes flashing. 'If we're to have a good working relationship, Mr Sawyer,' she snapped, 'then I think you'll agree that it's best if we keep our interests strictly professional.'

His black eyes glittered dangerously. 'Believe me, my interests are professional!'

She bit her lip in confusion. 'I'm not up for grabs, Mr Sawyer. I don't sleep around. I believe that's the expression used,' she added primly.

He grinned. 'It doesn't hurt to humour the boss, surely?'

'The only way I'll be humouring you, Mr Sawyer, is by working hard at my job!'

'If you call me Mr Sawyer one more time I'll throttle you!'

'Do you always resort to threats when you don't get your own way, *Mr Sawyer*?' she asked sweetly.

He grabbed her arm, pulling her towards him,

black eyes smouldering. Sarah trembled as she stared up at him, her heart hammering in her chest.

'One thing you can count on, *Miss Ames*,' he growled softly, pulling her still closer, her breasts pressed against his chest, his mouth hovering above hers. 'I *always* get my own way!'

'Yes, I've heard that about you,' she boldly dared to say. 'Tell me, Mr Sawyer, do you fire women if they refuse to give you what you want?'

He smiled down at her, a smile which chilled her to the bone, but still she kept her ground, refusing to be intimidated by this man. She didn't blink an eyelash, her gaze as cold as his was hot. 'I've never been refused; quite the contrary,' he bit out.

'Well, this is a first, then. No wonder you're taking it so badly.'

Her nostrils were filled with the clean male scent of him, her breasts tingling against his chest. If he didn't let her go, and soon, her body would betray her, and once he realised she was physically attracted to him the way he seemed to be with her, then there would be no stopping him, that she knew. She glared defiantly up at him, her body rigid against his.

'I could take you now and you would enjoy it.'

'How dare you say such things to me?'

His grip on her relaxed and she breathed easier. 'I'm willing to give you time to adjust to the idea of my making love to you.' His hands slid down her arms, sending shivers throughout her body. 'Because I fully intend to do just that!'

'Even against my will?' she gasped. 'You ... you would actually r-rape me?'

'It won't be necessary,' he drawled, enjoying himself now. 'I'll know when you're ready.'

'Never!' she cried out. 'You're wasting your time with me. Pick on somebody else.'

'But I've already picked you. You should feel flattered. A lot of girls would envy you.'

'My, but you're conceited! I could never feel flattered by any attention you showed *me*! I only wish jobs were more plentiful, easier to find, because I would love nothing more than to say to you right now that I don't want your job!' She was shaking with agitation, her eyes flashing with contempt, the red-brown plait draped over one shoulder, tiny wisps clinging damply to her flushed cheeks.

He reached out and grabbed her plait, pulling her gently towards him. 'It excites me when I see you getting yourself so worked up,' he drawled smilingly into her upturned face. 'It proves you want me.'

'No!' she gasped.

'Yes!' He bent his head, lips tantalisingly close to hers, tempting her with the potency of his charm. Sarah squeezed her eyes shut, the only defence she could think of under the circumstances. 'You can't hide from me, Sarah. Open your eyes and stop behaving like a child. Open

them, or I'll kiss you, and I won't stop with just
that, I can assure you!'

She reluctantly opened them, glaring up at
him, chin raised defiantly. 'Threats!' she
snapped. 'That's all you can do, threaten me.'

Black brows rose mockingly. 'I agree,' he said
throatily. 'Perhaps action is what you want.
Perhaps you enjoy being difficult . . .'

'Me!' she shrieked as she pushed ineffectually
against his chest. 'You're the one who's being
difficult. All I want is to go h-home.' She looked
appealingly up at him. 'Please, if you let me go
now I promise I will forget this ever happened. I
won't hold it against you, I . . .'

His deep-throated laughter stopped her and
anger flared like a white-hot torch within her as
she realised he was actually laughing *at* her. Oh,
he was insufferable! She pulled back her foot and
kicked him hard on his shin. The laughter died in
his throat while surprise blazed in his eyes. He
had dropped her plait, which was what she had
intended, but for some perverse reason not
known to herself she didn't run from him.
Instead she stood her ground, smiling at his look
of rage, enjoying her small victory.

'Ooops, sorry, Mr Sawyer,' she taunted. 'My
foot slipped. I'm not usually so aggressive, but
under the circumstances I trust you will
understand.'

To her astonishment he threw back his dark
head and roared with laughter while Sarah stood
quietly in front of him, puzzled. This wasn't

quite the reaction she had expected, but she was relieved all the same. His laughter seemed to wash away the tension between them, and she felt herself relaxing.

Finally he placed his hands on her shoulders, shaking his head. 'No one, male or female, has ever had the nerve to stand up to me before. It's a new experience and one I'm not quite sure I like but at least it's interesting.' He gazed steadily into her startled green eyes. 'Extremely so!'

Sarah eyed him warily. What was he up to now? she wondered suspiciously, refusing to acknowledge that his devastatingly charming smile was beginning to affect her nervous system. He slipped an arm around her shoulders and she immediately stiffened.

'Relax,' he taunted softly. 'My mind is strictly on business now.' He smiled down at her. 'How would you like to see your office?'

'Now you're talking,' she grinned happily, stepping neatly from under his arm and flicking back her plait. 'I'd love to see it.'

He chuckled and opened the door leading on to the assembly area. Sarah followed, listening attentively as he described what each area was for, hearing the ring of pride in his deep voice as he told her how not so many years ago he could have fitted his whole operation into one tiny section of the huge assembly area.

'I started off in an old tin shed behind a jewellery shop. My apprentice was older than me and he now runs my southern operation. Kirsten came in twice a week to do typing and filing and generally keep the place tidy.'

He stopped talking, and Sarah saw a faraway expression in his eyes; she wondered if he didn't sometimes yearn for the good old days when his life must have been a whole lot simpler. The look disappeared as quickly as it had come, replaced by a burning fierceness which she suspected had driven him to such formidable success.

'Now for your office,' he said almost curtly, leading her out of the area and down a long corridor, opening a door. 'How do you like it?'

Her own office! She looked happily around. She had wondered which of the offices would be hers, and now that she knew it was this one, decided it was by far the best of the lot.

'It's beautiful!'

He lounged against the door, feet crossed at the ankles, obviously enjoying her pleasure as she moved about the room examining everything in detail. The walls were painted a creamy beige, the carpeting and filing-cabinets copper-coloured while her desk was a burnt orange, the chair behind it of the same colour. She had her own white telephone and on her desk was a small television set. Sarah ran her fingers across the dials and then looked up at him questioningly. He chuckled and moved towards her, flicking one of the knobs. Immediately the plant came into view; the assembly and storage areas, and, with another flick of the knob, the infirmary.

'This knob, when pushed down, allows you to

speak to anyone you wish to in each of these rooms,' he explained. 'For instance, suppose there's something you need to know from the plant manager but you can see from the screen that he's busy on the other side of the room, away from the phone. Instead of disturbing him, if the matter isn't urgent, you can either wait until he's finished or you can see which phone he's closest to and press the appropriate button. Saves a lot of unnecessary running around.'

'Yes, it would.' She frowned. 'It's sort of like a spying system too. The employees must feel Big Brother is watching them!'

He shrugged. 'I doubt that. The system has worked very well in my other plants. The staff appreciate it. Apart from their wages, each receives an incentive bonus for parts assembled, so you can see any time I can save them is money in their pockets.' He quirked one dark brow. 'And I certainly don't expect you to sit here watching them all day! You'll have work of your own to do.'

Sarah flushed a deep red. 'Of course! I didn't mean me!' She glared up at him. 'I meant *you*!'

'You really do like to see me in the worst possible light, don't you?' he drawled with a mocking smile. His eyes trailed over her slender body, resting a fraction too long on her uptilted breasts before moving slowly downwards. She knew he was deliberately trying to unnerve her so she willed herself to remain calm, pretending not to notice that he was practically undressing her with his eyes. She leaned against the desk, hands resting on the edges, mocking him in return.

'I don't like to see you at all,' she taunted, meeting his dark gaze with bland innocence. She moved quickly away from the desk towards the large picture windows, her pulse-rate dropping dramatically now that she was at a much safer distance from him. She parted the lovely beige curtains and gazed silently out at the newly landscaped gardens, taking this time to regain her composure.

He *is* my boss, she was thinking, and no matter how much I dislike him I must try to get along with him. He had given her this job, but he could just as easily take it away. She must *force* herself to be nicer, to behave more like the employee she was than the sparring partner she had unwittingly become. For the sake of her family she must at least *try*!

She swung around to face him, her breath catching in her throat at the ruggedly handsome picture he made standing next to her desk, an unreadable expression in the blackness of his eyes. His hands were thrust deeply in his pockets, dark head slightly lowered as he stood silently watching her, the handsome curve of his mouth drawn into a tightly forbidding line. It didn't come as a shock to see that he was angry.

'These curtains are beautiful,' she murmured, picking up a fold of the soft beige material. 'It allows the natural light to flow in, yet it screens the sun. You should have seen some of the places I went for interviews.' She chuckled softly, and shook her head. 'Hideous, some of them.' She looked down at the material in her hand. 'But this, this is truly *magnificent*!' She smiled charmingly across at him. 'Did you choose it yourself?' she enquired sweetly, hoping she wasn't going overboard in her praise.

Angus pushed himself away from the desk and crossed over to her. 'You're patronising me,' he growled, taking her hand and removing the fabric. 'I didn't choose it nor do I think it could be classed as magnificent. It's standard material for most offices, plain but functional.'

Sarah sincerely hoped her cheeks weren't as red as they felt. 'I don't think they're plain,' she mumbled, detesting the look of amused mockery in his dark eyes.

'No, you think they're beautiful,' he said softly, placing the back of his hand against her hot cheek. 'You've gone to great pains to convince me of this.' He smiled roguishly down at her. 'You're trying to please the boss!'

Sarah swiped his hand away. 'I'm just trying to get along with you, that's all,' she stated mutinously.

He chuckled softly, his dark eyes holding her own fiery green ones. 'Don't think you have to be *nice* to me to keep your job,' he surprised her by saying. 'I hired you on your merits, as I do any of my staff, and you will only be kept on if you do your job well.' His voice took on a gentle quality, and she saw by his eyes that he was sincere. 'A good employee is always hard to find, but I think in you I have the very best!'

Sarah's cheeks flushed with pleasure and her smile was radiant as she said, 'Thank you, Mr Sawyer. I really needed to hear that, I . . .'

'There you go calling me Mr Sawyer again.' He sighed mournfully and Sarah laughed happily, knowing he wasn't in the least bit annoyed. Her eyes were sparkling as she gazed around her office.

'I can't believe it's mine,' she said. 'Everything is so modern and beautiful. I just wish my family could see it.'

He was watching her closely, half amused, half puzzled by her obvious delight. 'Your family can come around any time they like. I certainly don't mind.'

She sighed and the animated smile died slowly from her face and her beautiful eyes clouded with despair.

'They can't,' she said. 'They live too far away.' She took another look around, and Angus Sawyer knew she was committing every detail to memory. Her family might not be able to see for themselves, but he had no doubt they would know exactly what Sarah's work place was like. He looked at the curtains and smiled before placing his arm around her shoulders.

'Come on,' he said gruffly. 'Unless you want to see anything else I'll lock up and then we can go.' He smiled down at her upturned face. 'I'll drive you home.'

'Oh, no,' Sarah answered quickly, more disturbed than she ought to have been by his arm around her. 'I don't want to take up any more of your time.'

'Nonsense,' he stated, releasing her and walking towards the door. 'Wait here while I lock up. I'll only be a minute.'

'No, please, Mr Sawyer,' Sarah called after him. 'I prefer taking the bus. I want to see if it follows the same route back.'

He stood with his hand on the knob and studied her in silence for a few seconds. 'You can find out tomorrow. Right now you look tired.' He opened the door. 'I'm driving you home.'

Sarah knew there was no point arguing with him. Besides, it would seem foolish and churlish not to accept his offer and she was tired. How observant of him to notice, she thought with some surprise.

'All right, thank you,' she murmured, crossing the room to join him by the door. 'But there's no need to come back for me. I'll go with you. Your car must be parked out behind somewhere.'

'It is,' he agreed, allowing her to pass through the door before closing it after himself. 'Nervous about tomorrow?' he asked as they walked down the long corridor, the odours of fresh paint and plaster mingling pleasantly in the air.

'A bit,' she admitted. 'But I suppose I shouldn't be. After all, I am fully trained,' she added with a small degree of self-importance.

'Ah, yes, the college graduate!'

Sarah flushed at his tone. 'I should imagine you've a few degrees to your credit.'

He shrugged. 'A few.' He stopped at one of the closed doors and swung it open. 'This is the office manager's office. It's not far from your own.' He smiled mysteriously down at her. 'Just a short, *safe* distance away.'

Sarah frowned, a trickle of uneasiness creeping along her spine. 'What do you mean by that?' she asked, running the tip of her tongue nervously across her lips.

'Oh, it sometimes happens that managers are a trifle hard on their assistants,' he answered teasingly, doing nothing to relieve Sarah's sudden feeling of foreboding.

'And . . . and do you think that will happen to me?'

'No, I think you could handle whatever comes your way.'

Sarah took a deep breath. 'I'm sure I can.' She took another deep breath. 'After all, as long as I do everything right he should have nothing to complain about.' She looked up at Angus for reassurance but found nothing reassuring about the amusement glittering in his black eyes. She stepped past him and entered the office.

She saw immediately that the office manager was held in high esteem. Although the office was similar to her own, it was much bigger and far more elaborate. Her eyes took in at a glance the white furnishings, the framed pictures on the walls, the plush sofa and chairs and the coffee-table already stacked neatly with up-to-date magazines. It looked more like a reception room than a work-room, Sarah couldn't help but think.

'Jealous?' Angus taunted from the doorway.

'No, I love my office,' Sarah answered truthfully, ignoring his taunt. 'This is certainly stylish, though.'

'Someday it could be yours.'

'Better not let the office manager hear you saying that,' she laughed. 'He'll think I'm after his job, and *that* could be dangerous!'

'What makes you so sure it's a *he*? It could be a *she*!' He leaned against the door frame, ankles crossed. 'After all, you applied for the position yourself.'

'Don't remind me,' she groaned, remembering her encounter with Kirsten and how if it hadn't been for Angus's intervention she wouldn't be standing here right now. She was glad Kirsten worked at the head office in town and not here at the plant. Their personalities clashed, to say the least.

'Well, someday this office might be yours,' Angus repeated as they stepped from the office and closed the door. 'I like to promote within my firm whenever possible.' His black eyes gleamed down at her. 'Of course you must work hard and do as you're told!'

'So long as I'm able to do my job without

interference from ... anyone,' Sarah replied stiffly.

'Meaning me?' he enquired innocently, grabbing her plait and giving it a gentle tug before allowing it to drop across her slender shoulder.

Of course she meant him! Who else had the talent of getting under her skin the way he did? And she wished he would leave her hair alone. Hadn't he ever seen a plait before? Goodness, every time he touched it, her scalp tingled! It was terribly annoying.

'Of course I don't mean *you*, Mr Sawyer,' she answered sweetly, large green eyes rounded in innocence as she gazed up at him. 'You wouldn't want to waste my precious time when you're the one paying such a handsome salary!'

His deep-throated chuckle sent shivers down her spine. 'Time spent with you certainly wouldn't be wasted!'

Sarah ignored the suggestion in his voice, and when he realised she wasn't about to be goaded he chuckled again and, whistling softly, went about the business of securing the plant while Sarah watched.

With the plant safely locked up Angus took her arm and led her out to the car park. Her eyes widened at the sight of a long, low, gleaming red Maserati. It looked fast and dangerous.

'I'm not getting in that thing,' she declared, stepping well back from it. 'I prefer the bus. At least I'll know I'll get home safely.'

'You have nothing to fear,' he said, opening

the door and waiting for her to get in. 'I'm a very good driver.'

Sarah hung back. 'I'm sure you are, but . . .'

'No buts allowed,' he said taking her firmly by the arm and steering her into the low seat. He crossed to the driver's side and slid in beside her. 'Relax. You'll enjoy it.'

And surprisingly, she did. True to his word, he was an expert driver, weaving the vehicle effortlessly through the traffic. The top was down and the cool air fanned her warm cheeks and tossed her plait around her face, making them laugh.

'I'll have to tell Billy about this,' she shouted above the wind. 'He'll be very impressed.'

A dark frown marred Angus Sawyer's handsome features. 'Who is Billy?' he demanded to know.

'My kid brother. We live on a farm in the outback and the fastest thing he's ever been in is an old ute.' Her eyes sparkled up at him. 'Will he be jealous!'

Angus relaxed beside her. 'Perhaps some day I'll give him a ride.'

'Oh, he'd love that.'

'I might even let him drive it himself.'

'Heavens, no.' Sarah was horrified. 'He would *kill* himself!'

Angus chuckled and pressed his thigh against hers. 'Don't worry,' he drawled. 'I would give him plenty of instruction first, and I'd be sitting right beside him.'

Sarah moved towards the door away from his disturbing closeness. Did he really think that by offering her brother a ride in his sleekly expensive sports car it would be enticement enough to allow him liberties with her?

'The occasion will probably never arise,' she responded airily, and in the same breath told him her street number.

When he pulled up alongside her flat and looked enquiringly down at her Sarah knew he was expecting an invitation to accompany her inside. She almost hoped he would ask so that she could have the pleasure of refusing.

To her disappointment he reached across her and opened the door. 'Good luck tomorrow,' he said cheerfully, and there was nothing for her to do but to step from the vehicle.

'Thank you for the lift home,' she said almost shyly.

'My pleasure.'

'It's a beautiful car.'

'I like beautiful things.'

'Yes, well . . .' Why didn't she go in? What was she doing standing here fumbling for words while he sat in the comfort of his car watching her with amused mockery in his dark eyes.

'I'll see you tomorrow,' he said softly, starting up the car's motor.

'You'll be around at the plant then?' Goodness, did she have to sound so darn grateful?

'Yes, for a while, in case there are any

problems which need sorting out. New plant, new problems.'

Her cheeks dimpled into a smile. 'Yes, I suppose there would be.' She hitched her bag higher on her shoulder. 'See you tomorrow.'

The plant was a bustle of activity when Sarah arrived the next morning. She spotted Angus immediately and he looked every inch the businessman, dressed in a smart three-piece business-suit, his crisp white shirt startling against his deep tan. Her heart almost stopped beating when she saw who he was with. Ten minutes later he entered her office.

'Good morning,' he greeted her, his dark eyes moving appreciatively over the shining waves of her hair and down the elegant lines of her navy-blue dress.

'The same to you,' she smiled. She took a deep breath. 'I saw you with Kirsten. I suppose she's here to take notes for you?'

'Not at all. She's here because here is where she belongs. Kirsten will be your boss.'

'You mean . . . you mean . . .'

'That's right,' he drawled wickedly. 'Kirsten is the office manager!'

CHAPTER THREE

SARAH stared up at him from her desk, its smooth surface piled high with files. Angus was teasing her about Kirsten. He had to be.

'I don't believe you,' she said, smiling at his joke. 'You're trying to unsettle me, that's all.'

'Now why would I do a thing like that?' he drawled, returning her smile.

'Because you're mean?'

He chuckled and moved closer to her desk. 'You'll like Kirsten once you get to know her. She's tops at her job. There's nothing she can't do.'

'So it's true then? She really is the office manager?'

'That's what I said.'

Two hot spots of colour appeared high on Sarah's cheeks. 'Why didn't you tell me yesterday?'

'You didn't ask.'

'Well, that's because I assumed it wouldn't be anyone I knew,' she replied heatedly. 'You deliberately kept that information from me.'

He frowned darkly. 'Yes, I did,' he surprised her by admitting. 'I knew you were nervous about starting today and I saw no point in adding to that by telling you about Kirsten.' He sighed deeply. 'I'll expect the two of you to get along, and I'm sure you will do your part in seeing that you do.'

Sarah heard the warning in his voice and wondered if he had issued the same command to Kirsten. She took a file and opened it. 'I'll start right now,' she said, her fingers deftly sorting out the pages contained in the folder.

'That's my girl.'

She looked up from her work. 'I'm not your girl!'

He placed his hands on the desk and leaned towards her. Amusement danced in his eyes. 'Don't be so prickly,' he chided. 'It's just an expression.'

'And one I've never particularly liked,' she answered primly, shutting the folder and reaching for another. 'It's so belittling,' she continued as she worked. 'In one of the jobs I had during my holidays a manager kept referring to his forty-year-old secretary as "my girl". I'll get my girl to type it; I'll have my girl run it over to your office; my girl will make us a cup of coffee.'

Angus laughed and pushed himself away from the desk. 'I get your point, and I promise never to call you "my girl" again although I meant it in quite a different manner from what you've just illustrated.'

Sarah bent her head over the files. 'Now that Kirsten is here, I suppose you'll be looking for someone for your downtown office.'

'That's already been decided.' He shoved his

hands into his pockets. 'Or were you hoping for the job?'

'Certainly not!'

'It could still be arranged. In fact I've already thought about it. You would see a lot more of me.'

Sarah's eyes widened in astonishment. His conceit was truly amazing. 'Thanks, but I have an excellent memory. Whenever I feel I can't stand another second without seeing you I'll conjure up your image. That should be enough to keep me going.'

There was a flash of white teeth as he grinned. 'You won't be needing a photograph, then?'

'I hardly think so.' She closed the folder with a snap. 'Surely you have something better to do than stand there and watch me work on these files.'

'I'll go if you promise to have lunch with me.'

'I don't know when my lunch hour will be.'

'Make it twelve.'

Sarah hesitated. 'Kirsten might have other ideas.'

'I'll arrange it for you.'

'No, I don't think that would be a good idea,' Sarah answered slowly. 'You might own the place, but you will only be around for a few days. I think it's important not to ask for favours so early in the game. I want my working relationship with Kirsten to get off to a good start.'

He smiled at her seriousness, but Sarah had the distinct impression that he approved of her decision, even if it meant he might be without her company for lunch.

'What about *our* relationship?' he asked softly.

'I wasn't aware we had one,' she answered directly, looking him straight in the eye. 'You won't be at the plant and you're not my boss, so ...'

'I'm not talking about working relationships,' he cut in suavely. 'There are other relationships we could have.' He circled the desk and stood behind her and Sarah stiffened when she felt his hands on her shoulders, his touch light and caressing and strangely exciting.

'I was thinking of a loving relationship,' he said, his voice a seductive drawl as he parted the hair at her neck and lightly kissed the tender skin of her nape, sending wild shivers throughout her body. 'I'm told I'm an excellent lover.'

Sarah jumped up from her chair, whirling around to face him while green daggers shot from her eyes. 'And you need to be told that sort of thing?' Her cheeks were flaming from his outrageous statement. 'Yes, I can imagine you expecting to hear compliments, even when you're in bed.' She picked up a file and held it in front of her like some sort of protective armour, and surprisingly it worked. She felt calmer, less intimidated by his imposing height and disgusting good looks. 'You need that sort of reassurance, do you?' Her glance was questioning, her smile sympathetic.

Anger flared briefly in his dark eyes while a

deep hue spread swiftly across his high cheek-bones. Sarah experienced a thrill of triumph that her words had managed to dent his male ego. Her victory was short-lived, however, when he threw back his head and laughed heartily.

'Ah, I'm going to enjoy biting that sharp tongue of yours,' he declared merrily, reaching down to tuck a silky lock of hair behind her ear while she glared mutinously up at him. He took the file she was holding, leafed through it briefly and then tossed it on to the desk. 'I'll see you later.'

Sarah stood staring at the closed door for several seconds after he had gone, wondering why his words had sounded more like a threat than a promise. However, her contemplation was short-lived when Kirsten came breezing into her office, looking every inch the business lady in her expertly tailored beige suit and with her blonde hair tucked neatly into a smart chignon. She was followed by two men dressed in white overalls, each wheeling a trolley with large filing-cabinets. Kirsten hardly spared her a glance before directing the men as to where the cabinets should go.

Sarah watched, first in amazement and then in horror, as her beautiful little office became cluttered not only with the filing-cabinets but also with a table which was installed in front of the curtained windows. Boxes were piled high on the table, and after the workmen had gone Kirsten turned to Sarah.

'Those boxes contain personnel files on all our employees,' she told Sarah. 'Most of the staff have been taken from other factories owned by Mr Sawyer. They're all highly trained in their field and chosen for their expertise. Mr Sawyer *always* starts off his factories with his very best people,' she added pointedly, and Sarah was left with no doubt that Kirsten considered herself to be one of the very best.

'Well, it certainly seems to pay off,' Sarah remarked smilingly, glad to know that Angus had included herself amongst the élite. 'He's extremely successful.'

Kirsten's cold blue eyes narrowed on Sarah's smiling face. 'Although in your case I think he has made a *terrible* mistake! We discussed the position of assistant manager, and I would have preferred someone older with years of experience. I only hope you don't waste my time and yours by constantly having to be told how things are done. If that proves to be the case I'll recommend that you be let go.'

'I'm sure that won't be necessary,' Sarah replied pleasantly, refusing to be intimidated by the older woman. She stood up and walked over to the files on the table. 'I take it these files are to be placed in the filing-cabinets just brought in?'

Kirsten snorted with annoyance. 'Of course. Where else did you think they would go?' She smiled at the heated flush on Sarah's cheeks. 'And I want new name tags made up for all of them. That should keep you busy for a few hours.' She marched over to the door. 'I shall be in conference with Mr Sawyer for most of the morning, and naturally we won't wish to be disturbed. Needless to say, a lot of important issues crop up when a factory the size of this one is first opened for production.' Her eyes flicked coldly over Sarah. 'Any questions?'

Sarah shook her head. 'Not at the moment, but ...'

'Good.' Kirsten opened the door, stepped through and closed it behind her.

'... but I would like to know when my lunch hour will be,' Sarah finished her sentence to the empty room. She sighed and looked around her. Her beautiful little office now looked like a storehouse for filing-cabinets. Her eyes moved slowly from the mountain of files on her desk to the boxes stacked with still more on the table. Her title might be Assistant Office Manager, but if Kirsten had her way she might very well find herself the filing-clerk!

Sarah worked steadily through the morning. She updated the filing-system using the latest techniques learned at the college. When Angus knocked at her door and poked his head in she had just finished and her cheeks were flushed with exertion and satisfaction.

'That's what I like to see,' he drawled as he walked over to where she stood by the row of cabinets. 'A hardworking employee who is obviously happy with her job.'

'Yes, I have enjoyed the morning,' Sarah

smilingly agreed. 'I've learned a lot about Sawyer Electronics just by sifting through these files. I feel I've been here four years instead of four hours! It's been very interesting, I must say.'

'Good, I'm glad to hear you say that.' He looked at the row of filing-cabinets which hadn't been there earlier.

'Hardly looks like the same old office, does it?' Sarah chuckled, following his glance to the table against the windows. It had been cleared of files and was now quite bare and looking out of place in the small office.

'Do you need that table?' Angus enquired frowningly. 'It takes up a lot of space.'

'Well, I suppose not now that the filing has been taken care of, although I couldn't have done without it while I was rearranging things.'

'Rearranging? How do you mean?'

Sarah spent the next half-hour explaining the new filing-system, how it worked and how much easier it was.

'I'm impressed,' he told her when she had finished. 'Kirsten set up the old system years ago and it's never been updated.' He smiled down at her, a very nice smile. 'New blood, new ideas, and all in one very pretty package!'

His compliment warmed her, although she felt a trifle uneasy about Kirsten. It had never occurred to her that Kirsten had set up the old system, but now that she had a chance to think about it she realised that of course Kirsten would have been the one. She had been with Angus since the beginning and was part of the old days. Instinct warned her Kirsten wouldn't be pleased with the change.

'The old system was good,' she said now. 'Perhaps I shouldn't have changed it.'

'Nonsense,' Angus growled. 'Any fool can see your way is the better method. Times change and most changes bring improvements.' He took the few steps necessary to reach her desk and flick on the indoor video. Immediately the plant came into view. 'Look at that,' he said and Sarah joined him at the desk, fascinated by the scene in front of her. 'Right now everything they're working on is the latest in modern technology. Tomorrow it could be out of date, obsolete.' He flicked off the set and looked down at her while she returned his gaze with open interest. 'See what I mean?' he asked softly. 'Unless we're willing to change, to accept new ideas and concepts, then not only are we out of the running but ...'

'Angus!'

Sarah and Angus looked up to see Kirsten standing in the doorway. Her beautiful face was carefully composed into a smiling mask, but only Sarah could see the effort it was costing her.

Angus glanced at his wrist-watch and frowned. 'Good heavens! Twelve-thirty already.' He looked enquiringly across at Kirsten. 'Is everyone assembled in the Board Room?'

'Yes, we've been waiting for you.' Still

smiling, she focused her gaze on Sarah. 'You can go for lunch now, but starting tomorrow your lunch break will be from twelve until one.'

'Thank you,' Sarah murmured, knowing Kirsten expected her to dismiss herself immediately. She reached for her shoulder-bag hanging from the back of her chair, but Angus intervened.

'I'd like you to come to the meeting,' he said. 'It's nothing formal, just a chance to air some ideas and iron out any problems. You'll enjoy it.'

Sarah knew she would. To participate at management level was nothing short of a dream. To be there when ideas were conceived, to see them through to fruition, to . . . She saw Kirsten stiffen and her enthusiasm waned. Kirsten quite obviously didn't want her at the meeting.

'And you don't need to worry about lunch,' Angus cheerfully added. 'Kirsten has arranged for sandwiches and coffee to be sent from the canteen.' He smiled broadly at both women. 'Shall we be on our way?'

Kirsten hesitated at the door which Angus was holding open for them. 'I don't think it's necessary, or even a very good idea for Sarah to join our meeting,' she said quietly to Angus. 'After all it is her first day, and she can hardly be expected to contribute anything.'

'Oh, but she already has,' Angus returned, casting an approving eye in Sarah's direction. 'She has completely overhauled our filing-system.'

Sarah's cheeks burned, and not even the frosty glance she received from Kirsten did anything to cool them.

'It was nothing really,' she murmured as Angus placed his hand on the small of her back and steered her through the doorway. 'I'll explain the method to you later, Kirsten and . . .'

'I'm quite certain that won't be necessary, my dear,' Kirsten returned coldly. 'As my assistant I will expect you to handle small jobs like filing.' She smiled up at Angus as they walked along the corridor towards the boardroom. 'Isn't it wonderful how new brooms always sweep clean?' While Angus chuckled at the remark, certain it was made in fun, Kirsten added quietly to Sarah, 'I wonder how long it will last!'

The Board Room was a long, low room tastefully decorated in soft beige furnishings with richly panelled walls. Several men were already seated in plush, comfortable-looking chairs, and the air was filled with their low rumbling chatter. They looked up when Angus entered followed first by Kirsten and then by Sarah. Greetings were exchanged and Sarah was warmly accepted into the family of Sawyer Electronics.

Angus took his place at a highly polished mahogany desk, not sitting behind it but standing in front in order to be closer to his employees. Sarah sat next to Kirsten in the semicircle of chairs.

The meeting progressed smoothly right from

the beginning. Angus brought out the best in his employees, listening attentively to their problems, expertly leading them to work out their own solutions. The results were amazing, and Sarah was beginning to see how he had managed to build such a vast empire in such a short space of time. His employees backed him one hundred per cent, and their loyalty shone from their eyes. There was nothing they wouldn't do for their boss and they knew their efforts would be returned tenfold. Angus Sawyer was their incentive, their leader, and they were his men.

They had had their sandwiches and coffee and the meeting was reaching a successful conclusion when Kirsten suddenly took the floor. She was worried about advertising costs, had almost exceeded her budget and what could she do? Sarah listened with mounting interest as Kirsten continued to talk. The file on advertising had been a big one, well padded with clippings from newspapers and magazines depicting the new plant and its products. There had been pages of television and radio schedules utilising prime-time viewing and listening slots. The amount spent had been enormous and Sarah knew Kirsten was right in being concerned. Used to a life of thrift where even one penny misspent was a crime never to be repeated, Sarah had been staggered by the costs and had wondered while she sorted through the file if the coverage had not been excessive.

'What do you think should be done, Miss Ames?' Angus asked.

Sarah stared across at him, hardly believing her ears. He was asking *her* for the solution! She nervously ran her tongue across her lips. He was lounging against the desk, feet crossed comfortably at the ankles, a curious expression in the deep dark hue of his eyes.

'Me?' she blurted, feeling the colour rush to her cheeks as he continued to hold her eyes.

He chuckled softly. 'Yes, you. You're sitting on the edge of your chair. I think you've already thought of a solution to the advertising problem.'

Sarah could feel Kirsten's hard blue eyes drilling into her, and while she kept her own eyes on Angus she was aware of being at the centre of everyone's attention. She rose slowly to her feet, something in the expression in Angus's eyes giving her the confidence she needed.

'Well, I might have a solution,' she began cautiously, her nerves not allowing her to hear the impatient snort tripping from Kirsten's clenched teeth.

'Yes, well, what is it?' Angus prodded gently when it appeared she wasn't able to continue.

Sarah took a deep breath. Get a hold of yourself, kid, she silently commanded herself. Here is your chance to prove your worth, to let them know that years and years of experience isn't always necessary, that ...

Kirsten had taken her seat when Angus addressed Sarah but now she rose to her full majestic height and her voice shattered Sarah's thoughts.

'I don't think Sarah is qualified to view her opinions at this meeting,' she said in a reasonable-sounding voice. Her eyes swept over Sarah and she smiled in false sympathy. 'Poor dear. You must be wondering if you haven't been thrown into the lion's den, this being your very first day on the job.'

But the lion's den, if that's what it was, was exactly where Sarah wished to be, and she met Kirsten's condescending smile with a grateful one of her own.

'No, I'm glad of the opportunity,' she said now, and her lovely green eyes swept back to Angus. 'Sawyer Electronics is a household name not only in this state but the other states as well. Kirsten has already mentioned that the advertising budget has almost been exceeded. Therefore I propose that all advertising be stopped for at least two months and ...'

'*Stopped?*' Kirsten's voice was a mixture of disbelief and fury. She looked triumphantly across at Angus and Sarah knew Kirsten wasn't alone in her thoughts. Judging from the expressions of the others at the meeting, it was evident they all thought the 'new girl' had either lost her marbles or hadn't had any in the first place.

'Please continue, Sarah.' Angus spoke softly, his quiet voice demanding that she be listened to. 'You were saying that all advertising be stopped for at least two months?'

'Yes,' she answered, then squaring her shoulders bravely continued. 'I realise of course the importance of advertising, but when a firm is as well known as this one then ... then ...'

Sarah looked helplessly around her. The men were viewing her with polite interest, while Kirsten was sending her a silent message to sit down quickly before she made an even worse fool of herself than she already had. Her eyes drifted back to Angus and he raised his black brows slightly; she took this as her cue to continue. She had come too far to back out now, he was telling her.

'I feel ... I think ... this plant could well afford to ride on the publicity Sawyer Electronics already enjoys. The momentum is there. It seems foolish to waste it,' she added simply.

She sat down. There was more she could have said, but it would only have meant stating the obvious. By stopping all advertising now the budget needn't go in the red, but the name would still be carried on in the wake of the publicity of other Sawyer Electronics concerns.

Sarah didn't hear the silence which followed her suggestions issued in such a clear and convincing voice. Her ears were ringing with the inner excitement she felt at having spoken up at her very first meeting. Even if her suggestion wasn't accepted, she knew it had been a reasonable and sound one. She hadn't disgraced herself and even if she had, at least she had tried.

Kirsten rose quickly to her feet. 'Yes, well,

now that my assistant has had her say I suggest
we return to the business of advertising. I've
arranged for our newest products to be shown on
prime-time television for the next three weeks.
This will be supplemented with radio broadcasts,
the breakfast shows and between five and six in
the evenings to catch the motorists.' She took a
breath. 'Due to the ever-increasing costs, I
thought we might limit our newspaper coverage
to the weekend magazine. The savings won't be
enormous, but they will be sufficient to keep us
from going too deeply into the red.'

Sarah studied her hands folded neatly in her
lap. It was obvious Kirsten hadn't found her own
suggestion to be a workable one. She stole a
glance at Angus. He was busily glancing through
the advertising file Kirsten had handed him, his
long brown tapered fingers deftly skipping
through the pages. There was a disconcerted
frown on his handsome features, the frown
deepening with every page he turned. Finally he
closed the file and placed it on the desk. When he
looked up the frown had all but disappeared, but
traces still lingered in his dark eyes. Sarah felt a
thrill of apprehension shoot down her spine.
Angus Sawyer had said he was a firm but fair
boss, and she had seen both sides during this
meeting. But there had been something about the
man as he looked through the file before placing
it on the desk and fixing them all with those coal-
black eyes, which made Sarah realise there was a
streak of ruthlessness which could make him an

extremely formidable enemy.

He looked directly at Kirsten. 'You were right to be concerned. Our advertising has reached saturation point!'

Sarah felt Kirsten stiffen beside her. Incredibly everyone else in the room drew themselves up in a sort of chain reaction. Inexperienced as she was, Sarah knew what was happening. *The chief wasn't happy!* His quietly spoken words had filled the darkest corners of the room just as surely as if a siren, followed by flashing red lights, had suddenly been thrown among them. The atmosphere wes electric, dangerous, and Sarah's mouth felt dry while every muscle in her body tensed, ready for action.

'I may have overdone it a little,' Kirsten nodded in agreement. 'But you've always stressed the importance of good advertising,' she added almost accusingly.

'And I see Sawyer Electronics has bought nothing but the best!'

Kirsten smiled. 'Of course!'

The smile slowly left Kirsten's mouth as Angus fixed her with cold, penetrating eyes. 'We'll follow your assistant's advice and stop all advertising for two months.'

Kirsten gasped. 'But ...'

Angus lifted his hand and this was enough to silence her. He turned to Sarah. 'You may leave the meeting now.'

Sarah was only too happy to escape. She busied herself in her office. Kirsten came in almost two hours later to warn her in tight-lipped anger that any future bright ideas were to be discussed with her first before being put forward at meetings. With the warning issued, Kirsten stormed from her office without a further word.

Sarah sighed and returned to her work. Her innocent suggestion at the meeting had widened the rift between herself and Kirsten. Kirsten had *said* she was concerned, but the Big Boss had asked *her* for the solution. The fact that it had turned out to be a darned good idea ...

Sarah smiled. I'm gloating, she thought. My first feather in my cap and I love the feel of it. When Angus comes in to congratulate me I'll shrug off his praises. I will be modestly humble in my hour of triumph and glory!

But Angus didn't come in to congratulate her. He left the plant shortly after the meeting and for the next month Sarah hardly saw him. When she did it was usually on television or in the newspapers, and she began to wonder what it was like to be constantly surrounded by politicians, bureaucrats, the rich and the famous. She wondered also if he ever grew tired of the adoring glances of the beautiful women who clung to his arm.

Not that she cared, of course. It was just something she wondered at, and usually it was when he made one of his infrequent visits to the plant to be treated with more of the same from his female employees.

Sarah always made certain her own voice was

coolly impersonal whenever he addressed her, and she rarely offered him a smile. She liked the fact that her behaviour puzzled him. He wasn't used to being politely ignored.

She was working on one of her assignments at the kitchen-table of her little flat one evening when the doorbell rang. A glance at the kitchen clock told her it was almost ten. Not expecting anyone, especially at such an hour, she approach ed the door with no small amount of caution.

'Who is it?' she demanded to know, standing well back from the wooden structure.

'Angus Sawyer.'

Relief mingled with excited anticipation as she ran towards the door and opened it. Angus stood there dressed in a dinner-suit and holding two plastic cups in his huge tanned hands. He didn't wait to be invited in but stepped past her into the lounge. Sarah caught a whiff of perfume and the faint odour of Scotch, and judging from his dress knew he and some female companion had spent the night on the town.

He handed her one of the cups. 'Coffee. Black with no sugar.' He sat down on one of the chairs and looked around. 'This is nice. Small but cosy.' He removed the lid from the cup, said 'Cheers' and took a drink.

Sarah stared at him. He was stretched out quite comfortably in the chair, long legs crossed, a look of deep contentment on his face.

'Ah, I've been looking forward to this,' he drawled, smiling up at her, his happy contentment reflected in his voice. 'Sorry it's so late, but . . .'

'But you had a heavy date and couldn't tear yourself away, right?' She took a deep breath. 'Why are you here?'

'To see you of course.' He patted the upholstered arm of the chair. 'Come and sit beside me,' he begged. 'And try to pretend you're happy to see me.' When she made no effort to join him, he sighed heavily and closed his eyes. 'Drink your coffee. It's getting cold.'

'No, you have it,' Sarah said placing the cup beside him on the table. 'I'm not the one in need of strong black coffee. You've been drinking!' she added disapprovingly.

He chuckled and peered at her through long spiky lashes. 'I would hardly call a couple of Scotches drinking.'

He settled himself more deeply into the chair, hands clasped behind his head, a sleepily seductive smile on his ruggedly handsome face. When Sarah looked pointedly at her watch he pretended not to notice and reached for his coffee.

'Well, don't make yourself too comfortable,' Sarah warned him. 'I don't want you falling asleep.'

He placed his coffee-cup down and rose slowly to his feet, his dark eyes never leaving her face. 'Do you want me to leave?' he asked quietly, reaching for her hand and drawing her gently towards him.

Sarah swallowed hard. 'You . . . you can finish your coffee first.'

'I've finished it!'

'Oh, well . . .' Her heart was thrashing wildly in her chest. 'I said you could have mine.'

He smiled into her clear green eyes. 'No, I've had enough.' His hand slid up her arm and around the slender column of her neck. 'I just want to spend some time with you.' He lowered his head and kissed her lightly on the mouth.

Sarah stepped back from him, her eyes clouded with anger as she touched her fingertips to her lips. 'Did your dinner companion turn you down?' she asked coldly. 'Or did you really believe a cup of coffee was sufficient to buy you a place in my bed?'

He shoved his hands into his pockets and looked broodingly down at her. 'Who mentioned anything about bed?'

'Why else would you be here?' she returned suspiciously, wishing now that she had kept quiet.

'To see how you were and to talk with you for a while.'

'Well, you've already done that, and you can see I'm fine.' She half turned away from him, her small shoulders slightly hunched with fatigue.

'What were you doing before I arrived?' he asked quietly.

'Working on an assignment.' She ran a slender hand through the thick mane of her hair and sighed. 'I'm having a bit of trouble with it. I can't get my columns to balance.'

'May I have a look?'

Her eyes lifted slowly to his face and suddenly she grinned. 'Are you offering to help me with my homework?'

'Only if I get a kiss afterwards,' he responded with a wicked gleam to his eyes.

Her grin worked into any easy chuckle. 'You drive a hard bargain, but I'm desperate enough to accept. But just a small kiss,' she warned him. 'And just one!'

CHAPTER FOUR

SARAH led Angus into the small kitchen where she had spent the evening working on her assignment. The table was covered with books, pens, pencils, a calculator and an old typewriter. In the centre of all this was a large white ledger-sheet neatly printed out with rows and rows of figures. She picked it up and frowned and sighed a weary little sigh.

'I've checked and double-checked my figures, but I can't get the darned thing to balance.'

'Let's have a look,' Angus said, taking the sheet from her and quickly scanning the figures.

Sarah watched him, thinking how his presence seemed to occupy the whole of the kitchen, and despite his obvious wealth how comfortably he fitted into her own modest life-style. He certainly looked divinely handsome in his dinner-suit and she found herself wondering who his date had been and what she had worn. Suddenly she wished she had changed into something a little more flattering than jeans and a T-shirt when she had come home from work. Angus spread the ledger-sheet across the table and leaned over it. Sarah watched, fascinated, as his long brown fingers skimmed over the figures. She could almost hear his brain recording and calculating like a human computer.

'Here's the problem right here,' he said, pointing to the column on the left-hand side of the sheet.

Sarah moved closer, her small shoulder touching his massive one as she bent forward. 'Where?'

'Right here. When you converted from imperial to metric you changed one thousand pounds to one thousand kilograms instead of what it should be, four hundred and fifty four and a half kilograms.'

'Oh, no!' Sarah groaned, thinking of the hours she had pored over the figures. 'How could I have been so *stupid*?'

Angus chuckled and reached for a small bottle of correction fluid. 'There,' he said after the final adjustments had been made on all the relevant columns. 'Your ledger is balanced.'

'Thank you, Angus,' she said simply as he screwed the cap back on to the bottle. He looked down at her and smiled.

'Say it again.'

'Thank you.'

He touched her cheek. 'I didn't mean that. Say my *name* again.'

She shrugged. 'Angus.'

'That sounded nice. Very nice. But say it once more and this time with a bit more feeling.'

'Oh, for goodness sake, *Angus*, must we stand

here all night with me saying your name over and over again?'

'You're right.' He cupped her warm little cheek in his hand and ran his thumb caressingly across her trembling lips. 'The hour is late and I can see that you're tired.' He drew her closer, black eyes holding green. 'Let's go to bed,' he murmured softly, 'and ...'

'And I can say your name there?' Sarah finished for him, slipping from his grip while she glared up at him. 'Or, once in bed, am I supposed to *whisper* your name?' She placed her hands on her hips and tossed back her hair. 'Do you know what intrigues me about you most of all?'

'My overwhelming charm?'

'Your disgusting conceit!'

He chuckled and placed his hands on her shoulders. 'You say the nicest things, and I guess that's what I find intriguing about *you*.' His hands tightened on her shoulders while a dark intensity grew in his eyes. Sarah felt herself being drawn irresistibly closer towards him and she remembered the kiss she had promised. Her arms slipped up and circled his neck, her fingertips brushing the thick black hair at his collar. He lowered his head; Sarah knew he was waiting for the kiss and she fought the urge to giggle. She stood on tiptoe, placed her hands on either side of his face and kissed him quickly before stepping well back. There was a blaze of triumph in her eyes when she saw the surprised disappointment in his own. Obviously he had been expecting more. Much more!

He ran his hand across his mouth and looked at her. 'That's it? That's my reward for doing your homework?' he asked mournfully.

'You didn't *do* my homework. You merely corrected an error, for which I've thanked you.'

He sighed and looked at the books scattered across the table. 'You work too hard,' he said glumly. 'How long have you been at this anyway?'

'Since I got home from work.'

'Why do it? You've got a good job. You don't need further study.'

'Why did you open up another plant?' she retaliated by asking. 'You didn't need to.'

He peered at her through hooded lids and then shoved his hands into his pockets. 'That's different,' he growled.

'Why? Because you're a man and I'm a woman?'

He laughed softly. 'I won't be drawn into that debate. No, with each new plant I open I create employment, whereas you're doing nothing more than tire yourself out.' He picked up one of her text books and read out the title. *Future Economy And What It Means* . He looked at her pale face, the tiredness in her eyes. 'Anything you want to know, you need only ask me.'

'Thank you,' she answered tautly, 'but I prefer to gain my knowledge through books.'

'And exhaust yourself in the process,' he

stated grimly as he began stacking the texts into a neat pile. When he had finished he straightened and gave her a long, considering look. 'I have some books you might find helpful. I'll bring them along to the plant tomorrow.'

'Well, thank you,' she answered in surprise, thinking he had changed his mind about her studies. 'I would certainly appreciate that.'

He silenced her with an impatient wave of his hand. 'Don't think I approve of what you're doing, because I don't. You're exhausting yourself, and if you're not careful you'll ruin your health. Working all day and all night is a certain recipe for disaster.'

A small frown puckered the smooth line of her brow. 'You sound as if you speak from experience. Were you once like me?' she asked, brightness creeping into her voice. 'I'll bet you were,' she continued softly, answering her own question. 'Yes, I can imagine you working twenty-four hours a day building up your business. What happened? Did you get sick and run down? I can't imagine *that*! You look *so strong, so healthy*!' She peeped teasingly up at him through the silky fringe of her lashes. 'Or was it your love-life which suffered? Did you have to draw the line at maybe two or three lovelies a week?' She sighed mournfully. 'It must have been tough.'

He glowered down at her. 'I'm not amused!' He lifted his hand and dragged it roughly through his hair and she smiled at the instant mess. 'Why don't you tell me to leave?'

'I was hoping I wouldn't need to, *especially* when you've expressed concern about how tired you seem to think I am.'

Whatever he had been about to say he obviously reconsidered, for his mouth clamped shut and he turned and headed down the short hallway towards the door. Sarah followed him, smiling at the broad expanse of his back and wondering if this was the first time Angus Sawyer had suffered a romantic rejection. At the door he turned, searched her face for any sign of a possible reprieve, found none and sighed.

'Good night, Sarah. Sleep well.'

'Good night, Angus. Thank you, I'm sure I shall.'

The next morning the telephone was ringing when Sarah entered her office. She picked up the receiver, at the same time noticing the stack of books on her desk.

'Good morning. Sarah Ames speaking.'

'Good morning, my little beauty.' Angus's voice filled her ear with his pleasant baritone. 'What did you think of the books I sent over?'

'I haven't had a chance to look through them yet, but judging from their titles they certainly seem suitable.'

'Good.' A pause. 'How did you sleep last night?'

'Like a log. And you?'

'Terrible! I kept having this ridiculous nightmare. You were surrounded by books and ledger-sheets making it impossible for me to get to you. I tried knocking them down but the darn things wouldn't budge. I feel worn out.'

'Poor soul.' She chuckled quite gaily, feeling not a shred of remorse. 'I guess you're just not used to sleeping alone. You were probably lonely.'

'And that doesn't make you feel sad?'

'Not in the least.' She reached across with one hand and removed the cover from her typewriter before shrugging out of the yellow blazer which topped her matching yellow sleeveless dress. 'I must go now, Angus. Thanks again for the books.'

'Hey, not so fast,' he growled. 'I need to see you. How about dinner tonight?'

'I don't think so.'

'You don't *think* so?' His sigh came across the wire and she smiled. 'What kind of an answer is that?'

'I have a seminar at eight. There wouldn't be time,' she explained.

'We'll make time. I'll pick you up from work at five o'clock.'

'I'd planned on doing a bit of reading before the seminar but . . . oh, all right, I'll have dinner with you,' she reluctantly agreed.

'That's my girl. Full of brightness and enthusiasm,' Angus softly chided.

She ignored his lightly veiled sarcasm. 'I must go now. See you at five.' She placed the receiver firmly but lightly down and sat smiling at the instrument.

'I'm *not* your girl, Angus Sawyer,' she said softly. 'A serious-minded, level-headed soul like myself could never possibly fall for a guy like you. A good-time guy! That's what you are, Angus Sawyer, and I don't believe for an instant that you lost any sleep over me last night.' She grinned broadly, shook her head in amusement and then started on the day's work.

It was almost lunch-time when Kirsten came into her office.

'How are things going?' she asked Sarah in her coolly impersonal voice.

'Fine, thank you.' She smiled brightly up at the older woman. 'It's a pleasure working here. Everyone is so friendly and helpful.'

'Yes, well . . .' Kirsten's voice trailed off when she noticed the text books on Sarah's desk. 'What are these?' she asked frowningly. 'Surely you're not doing school work during business hours.'

'Oh, no,' Sarah replied quickly. 'Angus dropped them off. He thought they might help me with some of my courses. They're texts from his old college days. I haven't even looked through them yet,' she added, rather unconvincingly because she had browsed quickly through the top one on Business Management.

Kirsten regarded her shrewdly through cold narrowed eyes. 'All right, but just don't turn your office into a classroom,' she warned, glancing disapprovingly from Sarah to the texts.

'I'm off now and I might not be back this afternoon. I have a business luncheon with Angus. There are several items I wish to discuss. Do you think you can manage on your own?'

Sarah smiled sweetly. She had spent the morning doing Kirsten's work, and judging from Kirsten's tone knew the older woman had no intention of returning to the office.

'I'm sure I can.'

'Make certain you do,' Kirsten replied coldly.

As Sarah had expected, Kirsten didn't make it back to work which meant Sarah had a double load for the afternoon as well. It also meant that Angus had forgotten about their dinner date. She tried to convince herself that she didn't care. In fact she told herself she was quite happy about it. The less she saw of Angus the better.

She decided there was no point waiting past five to see if he showed up, so when she was offered a lift downtown she accepted. Time saved by not having to wait for a bus meant she could have a light meal and prepare for her seminar. She would go to her favorite coffee-house located on the Queen Street mall where most of the students from the university hung out. The food was good, the prices reasonable and the atmosphere stimulating.

The mall was always filled with activity, and tonight was no exception. Sarah walked slowly along the coral-coloured pavement, soaking in the atmosphere. Buskers sang in groups while small crowds gathered to hear their original tunes. People tossed them coins and Sarah did too, tapping the toe of her shoe to their catchy, hand-clapping songs as she stopped and listened for a while before moving along to the coffee-house, her books tucked under her arm.

'Sarah! Sarah, wait!'

Sarah turned. Angus was rushing towards her, long legs quickly eating up the distance separating them. The evening was warm, typical of Brisbane's sub-tropical weather but Angus Sawyer looked as fresh and as cool as though he were surrounded by an invisible cooling unit. Dressed in white trousers and light blue short-sleeved shirt which showed off his dark colouring and muscular build, he held every female's eye as he made his way towards her.

'Hell, Sarah, you have a damned nerve!' he rasped, grabbing her shoulders, his fingers digging in cruelly as his black eyes bit into her face. 'Why didn't you wait for me?'

She was glad she had put her yellow blazer on, not because it was cold but with her books and handbag it was simpler to wear, and now hopefully it was preventing Angus's fingers from bruising her tender skin.

'I did wait.' She tilted her head, green eyes flashing defiantly. 'Until five past five.'

He muttered something under his breath and let her go. 'I was at the plant at five,' he insisted, 'I saw you leave.'

She held her books in front of her. 'I'm surprised you didn't shout after me the way you did now.' She glanced quickly around. 'People are staring at us. Do you usually make scenes?'

He grabbed her elbow and moved her along, dark head bent towards her. 'Let them stare, dammit, and yes, I'll make scenes if it's necessary to get your attention.' He reached for her books, relieving her of the burden. 'I feel like a bloody school-kid!' he muttered, and Sarah smiled at the fierce expression in his eyes.

'You sure don't look like one,' she said softly and he glanced into her eyes and his expression cleared, a rueful grin chasing away his angry frown.

'You're beautiful when you smile.'

'Only when I smile?' she teased, feeling reckless.

His grip tightened on her arm, only this time a wild shiver shot through her. '*Especially* when you smile, and *only* if the smile is for me!'

She laughed gaily. 'I should think you would hate having me smile at you all the time. Wouldn't it get boring?'

An intent look blazed from his black eyes. 'Never! Your smile changes with your moods. Only a poet could understand what I mean.'

They had stopped in front of the coffee-shop, students going in and out, each glancing curiously at the tall, handsome man and young, beautiful girl. Neither *looked* like students. Sarah would have been horrified to know they looked like lovers!

Her lips were parted, moist and inviting,

sparkling white teeth glistening, silky lashes brushing against satin-smooth cheeks, her slender hand raised to her head in a gesture of reluctant understanding, the blush spreading slowly across her cheekbones, telling him she was both pleased and flattered by his words. He drew in his breath and slipped his arm around her shoulders, noticing for the first time the coffee-shop. His reaction was both swift and disapproving.

'Why have we stopped here?' he asked, frowningly.

'For dinner. You did invite me for dinner remember.'

'Not here!'

'Yes, here.' This time she took his arm. 'Don't be such a snob. I eat here often.'

'Not when you're with me, you don't!' He started to move her away but Sarah held back.

'This time you're with *me*,' she said firmly, determined that he shouldn't get his way while he was with her!

He turned slowly and faced her, amused mockery glittering in his coal-black eyes. Sarah's heart thumped loudly and her throat felt dry. She didn't smile. She couldn't. He had read her mind and she felt foolish and incredibly naïve. But if she backed down now it would be worse. She held her ground and her look of defiance turned into a glare and his mouth twisted in a sardonic smile.

'I'm with you?' he asked softly and she

nodded, unable to tear her eyes from his. 'And this?' He turned and indicated the coffee-shop she had always loved but which now seemed terribly noisy and . . . good grief! what on earth had happened to the windows? Surely she would have noticed how *greasy* they looked. 'Is this where you wish to take me? Where you expect me to eat?' he finished, looking suitably horrified.

She grabbed her books from his arms. 'Yes,' she snapped, 'I knew you would hate it but it's just the sort of place I take *all* my dates!' She turned and marched through the doors, bumping into people as she went but totally unaware of this, not understanding why she should feel so hurt that he didn't like the little shop when really she *knew* he couldn't possibly like a place such as this. Not Angus Sawyer! Not *him*!

She reached the small table she usually sat at; the one in the corner away from the door which by now was generally understood to be hers, just as she knew which tables others preferred. In a way it was like a fraternity, a fraternity for the poorer, working students where they could get together and feel a common bond. People like Angus Sawyer couldn't understand this, nor were they welcomed. She would never have brought him here in a thousand years. It was just rotten luck that he had followed her, and worse luck that she had invited him in. What had she been thinking of?

Her chair was whisked out and Angus helped

her into it, taking her books and placing them on the floor. 'These tables are rather small, aren't they?' he complained, reaching for the grubby hand-printed menu and scanning through it. 'I think I'll try the "Special".' He glanced across at her. 'Snags and beans.'

The corners of Sarah's mouth turned up. She couldn't even manage to stay angry with him longer than a few minutes.

'The sausages and beans are nice,' she assured him, folding her arms on the table, 'but I think I'll have a salad.'

He passed her the menu but she shook her head. 'I have it memorised,' she laughed. 'It never varies. Even the "specials" appear when it's their turn.'

Angus put the menu down and glanced curiously around. Sarah followed his eyes. Small lanterns lit each table covered in red and white checked cloths. Young people clustered around them, some eating, some drinking, all chatting and trying to be heard above the noise of a guitarist, who was belting out her latest composition.

'Not your kind of place, eh?' Sarah asked, amused.

'It's not bad,' he reluctantly owned, 'but it's no place for a girl like you.'

'A girl like me?' she repeated softly. 'You hardly know me.'

His eyes held hers. 'Does anyone here know you better?'

She flushed at his tone. 'What do you mean?'

He reached across and placed his hands over hers. 'Is there a boy-friend watching us now?'

She snatched her hands away. 'Of course not. I told you I don't have time for boy-friends.' She became angry, surprising even herself. 'Don't you listen to anything I say?'

'I'm listening now,' he answered quietly, 'and I'm wondering why you're so upset.' He leaned back in his chair, eyelids lowered, nostrils slightly flaring. 'He's here, isn't he?'

It was a statement of fact, certainly not a question. Sarah frowned. 'Who?'

He leaned forward suddenly, causing her to draw back in alarm. 'Your boy-friend,' he snarled. 'Why else are you behaving so strangely? Why else did you not want me in here?' He grabbed her hands, imprisoning them in his. 'Is that why you dashed away from work?' Black eyes narrowed dangerously. 'You were rushing to meet him!'

'You're crazy!' she spluttered, trying to wrench her hands free.

His eyes swept again around the coffee-shop, probing, seeking out her lover. 'This is ridiculous!' He stood up abruptly, dragging her with him. 'We can't talk here.' He stooped and picked up her books, one hand still firmly on her arm. Sarah nervously wetted her lips, cheeks red with embarrassment as they became the centre of attention.

She allowed him to steer her out of the shop,

meek as a lamb, but once outside all fury broke loose. 'How dare you treat me like this in front of my friends?' she flared, her whole body bristling with anger. 'I shall never be able to come here again.' She stamped her foot in fury and frustration. 'I've never been so humiliated in my whole *life*! I could have *died* from embarrassment!' She tossed back her hair, green eyes flashing, cheeks still rosy. 'If you knew what I wished for you, Angus Sawyer,' she hissed venomously, 'you would be absolutely *terrified*!'

He stood quietly in front of her, a look of calm contemplation in his eyes. 'I think,' he drawled slowly when her tirade had stopped, 'you must be hungry.' He slipped a protective arm around her shoulders. 'You'll feel better once you've eaten.'

Sarah stared up at him, hardly believing her ears. He had spoilt the one place she could afford to go to enjoy a bit of social life. Already she could imagine what was going on in the coffee-shop, and no doubt she would be bailed up and made to explain who the handsome stranger was who dragged her out as if she were a teenage delinquent or something worse. Now he was behaving as if the whole thing were her fault; that she was hungry and it was her hunger which had caused her to lose her temper and that it had nothing to do with him. The man was insufferable and downright infuriating. Tears of exasperation filled her eyes. 'Oh, what's the use,' she groaned. 'Feed me if you must.'

He smiled down at her and his arm tightened around her shoulders. 'Poor thing,' he soothed, his hand stroking her hair. 'You need something hot and nourishing, and I know just where to go.'

He took her to his place.

CHAPTER FIVE

The Queensland Performing Arts Complex, on Brisbane's South Bank of the winding river, seemed like an island of golden light bathed as it was under the setting sun. The waterfalls and the many colourful fountains added to the fairyland splendour of the brightly lit bridges spanning the river. Neon lights flickered on the dancing waters, making it seem like a causeway paved with diamonds, sapphires and rubies. The view was spectacular, breathtaking, and this was what Sarah saw from the tiled terrace of Angus Sawyer's mansion situated high on the hills overlooking the river.

'Do you like it?' Angus asked softly, his eyes on her animated features as she viewed the fairyland below.

'I think I'm in love,' she whispered softly, her eyes never leaving the dazzling scene which constantly changed colours as the sun set deeper over the landscape.

Angus chuckled and put his arm around her shoulders, drawing her close. 'In love with a view?' he queried softly, his eyes holding the same fascination for her face as hers did for the view.

'Yes,' she continued in that same awestruck

tone. 'You are a lucky man, Angus, to have so much.' Her eyes turned slowly to meet his. 'And I don't think you appreciate any of it.'

His smile deepened at her seriously spoken words. 'Teach me to appreciate what I have, then,' he begged, a devilish gleam in his eyes.

Sarah moved out of the enclosure of his arms. From the terrace with its expensive outdoor furnishings she could see into the living-room. It was enormous. The original oil paintings alone must be worth a fortune. Soft music was piped out to the terrace, and she supposed it was coming from somewhere in there. A butler had greeted them and appeared not in the least surprised that his master had returned with a lady on his arm. How many 'ladies' had there been in his life? Sarah couldn't help but wonder. How many women had Angus brought to this beautiful mansion and stood at their side while they gazed at the view? Probably none of them had been so greatly impressed by everything they saw as she had been, from the moment the imposing structure had first come into sight until she had stood at his side on the terrace. He probably enjoyed showing the poor country girl what the city boy had to offer.

And Angus Sawyer, poor devil, had a lot to offer, there was no doubt about that. No wonder Kirsten was doing all she could to be part of his wealth. Sarah spread her arms along the terrace rail and shook her head sadly.

'I feel so sorry for you, Angus,' she sighed and

his eyes widened in astonishment at her sincerely spoken words.

'Sorry, for *me*?' He laughed with genuine amusement, but a strange light had taken residence in his eyes. 'Surely you jest?'

Sarah shook her head. 'You're all alone here in this huge mansion, yet you needn't be.'

'So true,' he murmured suggestively, moving closer to her. 'Why don't you move in with me? Your place is so small while this, as you've just mentioned, is huge. There's plenty of room for us both.' His smile was meant to charm and disarm her but it had the opposite effect on Sarah. She became angry.

'Don't you ever tire of saying things like that?' she snapped.

He shrugged his broad shoulders and looked at her with puzzlement in his eyes. 'What things? I only suggested what you wanted me to.'

Sarah stared at him. 'What *I* wanted you to!' she gasped. 'I wouldn't move in here with you if you *paid* me!'

'Then what *were* you suggesting?' he asked coldly.

'I was suggesting that you need a wife, a family. People you love and care about to share your life with you,' she blurted.

Dark brows lifted in sardonic amusement. 'And you think that someone should be you, right?'

'Certainly not!' she snapped.

'Then why make the suggestion in the first

place?' he glowered almost sulkily, shoving his
hands into his trouser pockets like a small boy
who for once hadn't got his own way.

Sarah smiled and resisted the temptation to
touch him. For the first time she realised how
vulnerable he was. His brilliance had created
great wealth and the power that went with it but
she doubted he knew the first thing about love.
He had never learned the difference between love
and lust. To a man like Angus Sawyer, they were
both the same. The only trouble was, you could
build a lifetime on one but not on the other.

'I made the suggestion,' she ventured slowly,
'because I care for you and I think your life-style
is all wrong. Every man needs a wife and family
and, despite your reputation, I don't think
you're any exception.'

A loud snort filled the terrace. 'Good *grief*,
woman! Who in blazes do you think you are
preaching to me like this?'

'I was only making a suggestion,' Sarah
answered primly, colour flooding her cheeks. 'I
might have known you would take offence.'

'Take offence!' he repeated with a bellow.
'Women are all the same. It drives them crazy to
see a happy single man! All they want is a noose
around his neck and a ring through his nose!'

'They look so cute that way!' Sarah returned
baitingly, her eyes flashing as angrily as his. And
to think she had been concerned with his welfare!
The man just couldn't be reasoned with.

He grabbed her hand and pulled her roughly

to him. 'And women look best when they're being made love to!' His hand reached up to her hair and he pulled her head back. Sarah opened her mouth to scream, but the sound died in her throat as his mouth covered hers. She struggled against him, terrified of his hands which were doing outrageous things to her trembling body.

'Keep still,' he snarled, his mouth briefly leaving hers to issue the command. Sarah caught a glimpse of his eyes and they were alight with fury. A terrified sob tore from her throat before his lips again claimed hers, bruising her, punishing her for daring to interfere with his life.

Her body caught on fire. One minute she was struggling against him as if her life depended on it and the next she was clinging to him for the very same reason. Sensation after sensation ripped through her, blotting out everything except the exquisite beauty of being in this man's arms.

Sarah could never remember afterwards when the cruelty ended and the passion began. Nor could she remember being carried to the wide terrace sofa where the twinkling stars danced to the strains of the music filtering through the living-room. She had vague memories of her dress being slipped from her shoulders, of the feel of hard lips on the erected peaks of her breasts, of experienced hands doing marvellous things to her body. It was only when she felt the weight of Angus's body on hers that reality returned with a rush.

'Angus! Please, no. No!' She sobbed out the plea.

'It's too late,' he rasped. 'I can't stop now!'

'*Angus!*' Her hands clamped down on the sides of his face as she frantically tried pushing him away.

With an agonised moan he drew away from her, rising to a sitting position as he dragged both hands through his hair. His cheeks were flushed with passion and his eyes were blazing with disbelieving anger and total frustration.

'First the advice then the lesson,' Angus declared thickly, watching in disgust as Sarah hastily straightened her clothing. 'What are you, anyway? A man-hater?'

He had reason to be angry, Sarah realised with a sickening heart. They had practically been at the point of no return when sanity had returned to her. However much this pained him, she was grateful their lovemaking had gone no further. Shame filled her. She should never have come here; it had been a dreadful mistake. She felt him stand up from the sofa, felt the glare of his eyes boring into her very soul.

'I'm sorry, Angus,' Sarah whispered as she slowly raised her eyes to meet his. 'I didn't mean this to happen.'

He drew in a ragged breath, his eyes never leaving hers as he did up the buttons of his shirt. Had she unbuttoned them? Sarah couldn't help but wonder, knowing she must have. It would have been so easy to blame her actions on him, but she knew she couldn't. She had wanted him every bit as much as he had wanted her. This knowledge troubled and confused her. She had known all along that Angus Sawyer was a dangerous man. Her instincts had given her fair warning about that, not to mention the man's reputation. She had already experienced what his touch could do to her. Even when he so much as glanced at her, her heart did strange and exciting things in her chest. No, she had no one to blame but herself and now she knew he hated her. His eyes were filled with loathing as he continued his silent appraisal of her.

Sarah bowed her head and rose slowly to her feet. She felt his hands on her shoulders, fingers digging cruelly into her soft flesh.

'Look at me, Sarah,' he commanded.

Sarah hesitated and then peeped cautiously up at him through silky lashes. The anger seemed to have left him, and in his eyes she thought she saw naked misery. Her insides shrivelled. He was tired of her, and who could blame him? Angus Sawyer didn't need to work for his loving! It came to him easily in every size and shape. Had it come to him that afternoon while he was with Kirsten? The possibility of this sickened her further. Why did he have to have so many women? Why couldn't they just leave him alone? Leave him to her!

Sarah shook her head in an effort to clear it from these ridiculous thoughts. Leave him to her indeed! She could never love such a man. Such a

man could never love *her*. They were worlds
apart in everything that mattered. She believed
in love and marriage, and he quite simply didn't.

'Forget what happened,' he quietly advised.
'No harm has been done, at least not in the
physical sense.' He straightened to his full height
and dropped his hands from her shoulders. 'I
believe dinner is ready. I hear Max with the
trolley.'

As if on cue, the butler appeared with a trolley
laden with food. Sarah watched as Angus helped
Max settle the tempting array of dishes on to a
glass-topped table. The butler smiled at her
before he made his exit, making Sarah wonder
whether the ageing gentleman suspected what
had taken place on the terrace. Angus turned and
indicated for her to join him at the table. Sarah
hung back. She didn't feel like eating, couldn't
possibly swallow food. She felt sick and she had a
tension headache. All she really wanted was to go
home, have a warm bath and sleep. She didn't
want to spend another minute with a man who so
openly disapproved of her Victorian morals.

'Sarah?' Angus impaled her with his gaze as he
stood stiffly by the table. 'Come and eat.'

Still she hesitated, not trusting her shaking
knees to carry her the distance to the table. Her
body felt warm, unbelievably alive, and as her
eyes met his across the terrace it was as if he was
still caressing her. She swallowed convulsively
and as he once again extended his hand to her,
her feet sprouted wings and miraculously she

was by his side, allowing him to settle her in a chair.

'I don't think I have time to eat,' she heard herself saying, hardly believing that the thinly strained voice could possibly be hers. It sounded as if the words had been squeezed through a tube.

'Nonsense,' Angus growled. 'It's barely seven and you said your seminar doesn't start until eight. You have plenty of time.'

'I had planned on doing some reading at the library first,' she answered in that same weird voice. 'It's what I usually do.' Heavens! She sounded like a lost child, pathetic and afraid. Get a grip on yourself, she silently commanded her vital organs.

'Stop worrying. We're not far from the university.' He placed some salad in a bowl and passed it to her. Sarah dutifully picked up her fork and began eating, keeping her eyes lowered so that she wouldn't have to look at him.

The meal was a silent affair. Sarah made no attempt at conversation and Angus seemed to forget she was even there. That rankled! She wondered what he was thinking about and if he was sorry now that he had invited her to his home. Her appetite in no way matched his own, but she did manage to do justice to the array of tempting dishes, from the tossed green salad topped with black olives, followed by avocado soup and spring chicken, straight through to the pavlova served with fresh strawberries, passion-fruit, pawpaw and moutains of whipped cream.

By the time Max served coffee, Sarah was totally mollified, this condition helped along by the two glasses of wine she had consumed. She leaned back in her chair and smiled as she watched Max carry the last of their dishes away.

'You're very lucky to have Max,' she told Angus, her voice soft now, her expression dream-like.

'You keep telling me how lucky I am,' Angus drawled, black eyes narrowed on her face.

'Well, it's true,' she insisted, her eyes meeting his. 'I hope you appreciate him.'

'I appreciate *everyone* who works for me.'

Sarah caught the enigmatic gleam in his eyes and hastily looked down at the coffee cup she held in her hands.

'Yes, I know you do,' she answered truthfully. 'And it pays off. Everyone is so loyal to you . . . to the plant. Do you know, hardly a day goes by that someone doesn't come in off the street wanting a job?'

'A sign of the times, I'm afraid. Unemployment is rampant.'

'No, that's not it at all.' She leaned forward, her expression eager. 'It's your reputation, Angus. People know they will be given the opportunity to learn, to be involved with experiments, to try their hand at design. You allow your workers freedom . . .' Her voice trailed off and she chuckled softly. 'Listen to me,' she said. 'I sound like some sort of crusader!'

Angus smiled and covered her hand with his. 'You sound like me,' he said softly, giving her hand a squeeze. 'Or at least that's what I vowed I would do when I opened my first plant.'

'But you do,' Sarah insisted. 'The opportunities are there for those who want to take advantage of them.'

'Not like in the old days, though,' he said thoughtfully with a frown. 'The "old days" used to mean thirty, forty, fifty years ago, now it can be last week or even yesterday. That's how quickly technology is changing.'

'Yes, but you're changing with it.'

There was no mistaking the ring of pride in her voice, nor the unshakeable faith she had in him, and a smile softened the hard lines of his mouth.

'It's not as easy as you might think, my sweet little Sarah. Today's project can end up in tomorrow's junk-heap along with the workers skilled in that particular field.'

'Is that why you allow your employees to have special projects of their own, then?'

'Yes, but within reason of course.' He shrugged and ran his thumb along the rim of his glass. 'It keeps up interest and nurtures that all-important ingredient, excitement!'

She nodded. 'Yes, boredom can be deadly.'

'And what about you, Sarah?' he asked quietly. 'Does the job still hold excitement for you, or are you beginning to feel the first destructive seeds of that deadly virus?'

'Boredom?' She shook her head, the soft chestnut waves swirling about her smooth cheeks. 'No, not yet.'

Black brows rose majestically. 'Not *yet*? Does that mean you will, eventually?'

Sarah laughed, the sound rich with undisguised amusement. 'Oh, Angus, if you could only see your face! Would it matter so much if one of your employees did become bored? Would you really take it personally?'

'Of course,' he growled menacingly. 'Boredom can be contagious. It spreads quickly and can be the major cause of poor workmanship and accidents.'

Sarah lowered her eyes in shame. He was right and she knew it. She had only been teasing, but he had taken her seriously. She knew she could never become bored with her job. It was far too diversified and exciting. She wanted to tell him so, but instead she heard herself asking, 'How was your luncheon date with Kirsten?'

She looked up. She had sounded *jealous*. Had he noticed?

'It wasn't a *date*! It was a meeting which involved lunch in order to save time. I have no romantic interest in Kirsten,' he assured her quietly. 'Why do you ask?'

'Just curious. Was anything important discussed?' she asked, managing to sound very businesslike.

A lazy grin spread slowly across his face. 'I

never waste time on trivia,' was his smooth reply.

Sarah put down her coffee cup and folded her hands in her lap. They were shaking. 'I really appreciated being invited to sit in on that meeting at the plant,' she said wistfully, and then could have yanked her tongue out. She had let him know by her tone that she felt left out because he hadn't invited her to the business luncheon.

'And I appreciated that suggestion of yours. We've saved considerably on advertising without losing on sales.'

'I've had other good ideas,' she promptly blurted.

'Why haven't I heard about them?' He smiled suddenly, those nasty male dimples doing wonderful things to his handsome face. 'You've been saving them for meetings?'

An embarrassed flush crept across her cheeks giving an attractive glow to her appearance. 'Well, yes, I suppose I have,' she admitted sheepishly.

'I'm always open to suggestions,' he said softly, 'and I've yet to turn down a good idea.'

She relaxed and leaned forward. 'Well, how does this sound? A computer club for the children of your employees?'

'We already have a social club.'

'I know. The annual picnic and the Christmas party. Fun enough for the parents and the younger children but not for the teenagers.

Apparently the only ones who attend are forced there by their parents.'

Angus frowned. 'I wasn't aware of that, but I guess it's pretty understandable. Teenagers usually have their own thing to do.'

'But what if they did their own thing at the plant? On Saturdays.'

'They would get in the way.'

'No, they wouldn't. There's no production going on, only the packers will be there. A space could be cleared for them at the back of the plant and you could give them all the bits and pieces left over from assembly. They could create things, and in the process become more aware of what their parents do for a living.'

Her enthusiasm was catching. Angus leaned back in his chair and formed a pyramid with his long tapering fingers, staring at them thoughtfully.

'That's not such a bad idea,' he said slowly. 'In fact it's a damned good idea!' His dark eyes shone on her face. 'I would have given my right arm to be let loose in a factory when I was a kid!' he admitted with such boyish enthusiasm that Sarah's heart did a crazy flip in her chest. The man could be downright appealing at times!

'Well, I don't think they should be allowed to run loose,' she laughed, adding in mock horror, 'Especially if any of them are like what you must have been like as a kid!'

He threw back his head and laughed and Sarah knew her suspicions had been correct. Angus

Sawyer had never been an angel!

'Do you know what appeals to me most of all?' he asked, serious now. 'Apart from giving the kids somewhere to go where they can play with sophisticated materials, it might also help solve some of the problems the parents are having with their kids.'

'Drugs, alcohol, that sort of thing?' Sarah asked quietly, her expression grave.

'Yes.' His expression became fierce. 'What sort of animal would sell drugs to kids? And why would kids take the stuff? They know how harmful it is, what it can and does do to them. They're educated against it in schools and on television; in fact practically everywhere you look or go there's some sort of campaign against it.'

'I know, but it doesn't seem to be doing any good. The problem is growing, and it all happened so suddenly. When I was a teenager, sharing a cigarette behind the toilets at school was considered rather daring, but now a great many children in primary schools are smoking a pack or more *each* a week!'

Angus shook his head. 'And by the time they're in high school they're hooked, or on to marijuana.'

'Yes; depressing isn't it?'

'Depressing and a heck of a worry for parents,' he agreed, watching her closely. 'You once mentioned a kid brother. Have you had any problems with him?'

Immediately she smiled and he saw the sudden loneliness which flashed briefly in her eyes.

'I have a sister too. Her name is Nellie. She and Billy are great kids. I don't think they would ever tamper with drugs. Apart from not having the money to buy any, they're lucky where they live. The availability of drugs in country areas isn't as great as in cities.'

'Well, let's hope this idea of yours helps some of the kids here.' He looked at his watch. 'It's time to go.'

'Oh dear, so soon?' She looked at her own watch. 'Yes, I guess I had better make a move,' she said, reluctant now to part from his company.

They stood up together and Angus went around to help her with her yellow blazer, carefully lifting her hair where it had become trapped by the collar. His hands felt warm against her tender skin and his nearness was intoxicating.

'Play truant tonight,' he murmured, turning her to face him, his hands resting on her shoulders while his dark eyes held hers.

'I'm sorry, Angus, but this seminar is far too important. I can't afford to miss it.'

He reached for her hands and pressed them to his lips. 'Please.'

She shook her head. 'Sorry.'

'Don't be mean.'

'If we don't leave right away I'll be late. How would you like that on your conscience?'

'Would they punish you?'

'She grinned. 'Fifty lashes.'

'Then we'd better not risk it,' he said as he kissed each rosy fingertip. 'You've got such beautiful hands.'

Sarah looked at her hands in his. They did look rather nice in his huge tanned ones! She withdrew them quickly and shoved them into the pockets of her blazer. This man's power over her was beginning to be more intoxicating than any drug.

'Shall we go?' she asked, her rising emotions making her voice sound cross and impatient.

He looked at her sharply. 'I'll get your books,' he replied coldly, adding, 'Obviously I've already wasted too much of your precious time!'

Sarah wanted to protest, to tell him she had enjoyed every minute, every second of her time spent with him, but somehow the words refused to come. Perhaps it was the dark forbidding expression on his handsome features which made her maintain her silence even as they made their way to the university and he dropped her outside the door. When she finally found her voice, the words which came out weren't quite what she had planned to say.

'I ... I enjoyed the ...'

'Yes?' he curtly prompted.

'... meal. It ... it was delicious.'

'I'll tell Max. I'm sure he will be pleased.'

It wasn't until the red Maserati had disappeared from her view that she finally said, 'But I

especially enjoyed your company. I enjoyed it . . .
a lot!'

Of course Angus Sawyer had no way of
knowing she had said *that*!

CHAPTER SIX

THE plant was deserted, the quietness eerie.
Sarah finished the last of the sales reports and
locked them in the filing cabinet. It was eight
o'clock, she was dog tired and her neck muscles
felt stiff and sore. She was also hungry, and she
wasn't looking forward to the bus trip home.

A muffled sound followed by several louder
ones filtered through from the back of the plant.
She stiffened with sudden fear then immediately
chastised herself. She was far too jumpy lately.
The security guards would be making their
rounds, checking locks on doors and windows.
Smiling away her foolish fears, she bent to
retrieve her shoulder-bag from the bottom
drawer of her desk. At that instant the door to her
office opened.

'Angus!' she gasped, one small hand pressed
against her pounding breast. 'Goodness, you
gave me a fright!'

'Obviously,' he scowled, dark eyes resting on
the small pale oval of her face, her beautiful
green eyes darkened with fatigue and fright.
'What are you doing here?'

'I was working on the sales reports,' she
replied breathlessly.

'They could have waited until morning.' He

glanced at his watch. 'It's past eight o'clock.'

'I know, but there was so much to do and . . . and . . .'

'And you thought you might clock up some overtime?'

Hot colour seared her cheeks. 'Of course not.' She took a deep breath and let it out slowly. 'It's easier to work on the figures when everything is quiet and there are no interruptions.' She slung her bag over her shoulder and held on to the strap, defiance blazing in her eyes. 'Did you want something in my office or were you merely making rounds?'

'I saw a light . . .' He didn't finish his sentence. Instead he shoved his hands into the pockets of his chocolate-brown trousers, the colour almost matching the deep tan of his skin, the crisp white shirt he was wearing a startling contrast.

'You saw a light and thought I had neglected to turn it off, is that it?' Sarah spoke angrily, circling her desk to stand in front of him. Her face was now the colour of the deep rose-pink dress she was wearing and her eyes were the colour of a turbulent sea.

He shrugged his broad shoulders. 'I thought it was worth investigating.' He pulled out his hand and touched her cheek. 'You're angry with me.'

She brushed his hand away. 'I'm not!'

'Yes, you are. You've hardly spoken to me since we had dinner at my place, and you haven't returned my phone calls. You're upset about something.'

'Don't be ridiculous,' she scoffed, tossing her head back and glaring up at him. 'How could anyone be angry with Mr Wonderful?'

'Mr Wonderful?' he repeated smilingly. 'Is that your secret name for me?'

'That's what I call you publicly. You wouldn't want to hear what I call you privately!'

His black eyes shone with amusement. 'I know what you mean. Publicly you're Sarah or Miss Ames, but privately you're the heroine of all my fantasies!'

'Victim would be more like it!'

He chuckled softly. 'Ah, you're even angrier than I thought.'

Sarah placed her hands on her hips. 'I tell you, I'm not angry! Just because you saw fit to leave me out of the planning for the junior social club is certainly nothing to get upset over. I'm sure you and Kirsten have everything under control and probably by now you've even managed to convince yourself that it was your idea!'

'So that's it!' He shook his head and chuckled. 'You're feeling neglected.'

'I'm feeling no such thing,' she huffed.

'Yes, you are, and I dare say your feelings have been hurt.'

'Well, you needn't sound so ... so *pleased*!'

'But I am. It shows you care about me.'

'It shows nothing of the sort.' She sighed heavily. 'I just can't understand why you won't let me help. It seems everyone else is involved except me.'

'And there's a very good reason for that.' He placed his hands on her shoulders. 'You've got your job and your studies. That's enough.'

'But I want to help.' She looked appealingly up at him. 'Please, Angus, I . . .'

His fingers dug into her shoulders and his expression became angry. 'No!'

'But why? It won't interfere with my work, I promise, and if I thought I was getting behind I would come in earlier and . . .'

'. . . stay later,' he finished the sentence, his voice grim. 'And that's exactly why I don't want you anywhere near the project. You're already over-committed.'

'I think I should be the judge of that,' she replied stiffly, turning away from him. 'Very well, then. If you don't want me that's fine with me.'

'You're being childish.'

'And you're being stubborn.' She whirled to face him. 'Stubborn and unreasonable.'

'Listen, Sarah, it's for your own good. You work too hard as it is. I swear you've lost weight and you're so pale. You even have dark smudges under your eyes. If you're not careful you will soon have *bags*!'

'*Ye gods!*' She placed a dramatic hand to her brow and closed her eyes. 'No wonder he doesn't want me near him. A thin, pale lady with bags under her eyes just isn't Angus Sawyer's kind of woman. How could I have been so *thoughtless*!' she wailed.

He grabbed the dramatic hand and held on to it, pulling her against his hard chest while she wrestled to free herself.

'Let me go,' she panted. 'You're hurting me.'

'I'm not and you know it.' He released her hand and smoothed back her hair from her face, his touch surprisingly gentle and completely unnerving her.

'I suppose you haven't eaten?' he sighed.

She shook her head. 'And I'm starving!'

'And I suppose you intended taking the bus home or are you going to make me feel better by telling me you've finally bought yourself a car?'

The corners of her mouth dimpled into a smile. 'Nope, no car yet.'

'I don't like you walking alone on dark streets and waiting at bus stops. It's not safe. Why haven't you done something about getting a car?'

She shrugged. 'It's quite simple really. I just can't afford a car.'

He frowned darkly. 'I might believe that if I weren't the one paying your salary.'

She lifted her dainty shoulders and dropped them. She had no intention of telling him what she did with her money. But he wasn't about to let the matter drop.

'Do you send money home?' he asked quietly.

The caring manner in which he asked the question brought the answer tumbling from her lips. She found herself telling him about the farm, their hardships, her father's death. The story was told simply, without any hint of self-pity. When she had finished there was admiration in his eyes. The Ames family were battlers and Sarah, whether she knew it or not, was their prize warrior. He sat on the corner of her desk and she sat next to him, marvelling at the warm sense of security his arm about her shoulders gave her. When he spoke she listened with the same attentiveness he had given her.

'In some ways our stories are similar. My father died when I was thirteen. I always thought we were rich but it wasn't until after the funeral that Mother and I learned Father didn't believe in paying his bills! Everything had to be sold to pay off the creditors. We ended up in a one-room flat. Luckily I was big and able to lie about my age. I took any job offered and when I wasn't working I was studying.' He shook his head sadly. 'Mother never got over the shock of Dad's death nor our financial situation. She felt personally humiliated and ... died three years later.'

Sarah picked up his huge tanned hands and kissed them. She wondered how big his hands had been when at thirteen he had started doing a man's job. Neither spoke. There simply wasn't any need.

And as Sarah sat next to Angus thinking about what he had told her she felt she at last was beginning to understand what drove this powerful man. She thought of what he must have been like at thirteen, this man-child who had suffered through the death of his father and had taken on full responsibility of a mother unable to cope. She pictured him struggling with jobs and schoolwork while he watched his mother's own personal heartbreak. No wonder he thought life was for the moment, that love and security just simply didn't exist or if they did, they could easily be snatched away. She reached up and touched his cheek and when he turned with eyes still haunted she smiled up at him.

'Thank you for sharing your past with me,' she said softly. 'And thank you for listening to mine.'

His expression gradually cleared. The light shining from her eyes was enough to chase away the ghosts. 'You're really something, do you know that, Sarah Ames?' he asked quietly, bending his head to kiss her gently on the lips. 'You're special!'

Her heart skipped several beats. 'I'm not so special,' she whispered between kisses.

'You're very special,' he whispered back, and it was then that Sarah knew what her heart had been trying to tell her all along. She loved him! Her heart sang for joy while butterflies danced in her stomach and fluttered up her throat. She swallowed hard and issued a silent plea for God to have mercy!

She was hopelessly in love with a man who had joked with the media that he would never marry. She remembered how she had smiled at his smugly arrogant statements but she wasn't smiling now. He must never learn about her feelings, she thought wildly, for surely he would take advantage of her tender love. Her name would not be included on his list of conquests. She believed in love and marriage while he quite simply and openly admitted that he didn't.

Sarah wrenched herself free and hopped down from the desk. 'Got to go,' she announced brusquely. 'My bus.'

He stared at her in bewilderment while she grabbed her bag. 'I'll drive you,' he announced in a carefully controlled voice as he rose to his feet.

'No, no, I'll take the bus.'

'Nonsense,' he snapped as he gripped her elbow.

Sarah was about to protest but one look at the tight, angry face looming above her convinced her now was not the time to stand up for her rights. Besides, she told herself as she walked meekly alongside him, she was tired and in no mood for riding buses tonight. It would be good to get home earlier than expected and ... Oh, what's the use of deceiving yourself, Sarah, she thought almost angrily and not without just a trace of self-pity. You're thrilled to be spending this extra time with him and you're even heartened by his concern for your saftey even though you know he would do the same for any of his employees.

She had expected him to take her straight home. Instead he pulled into a fashionable little restaurant nestled in a clump of Casuarina trees overlooking the river. Soft music greeted them as they stepped inside the cosy atmosphere and the delicious spicy aromas drifting through from the kitchen reminded Sarah she hadn't eaten since lunch.

Angus was greeted with all the enthusiasm of a favourite son returning from a long journey and without his even asking, they were escorted to a table for two which offered exquisite views of the river with its fairytale magic.

'Goodness!' Sarah remarked after the attentive waiter had taken their orders and another had filled their glasses with chilled champagne. 'I can't believe all the fuss they're making over us.'

'Don't you like it?'

'Well, yes, it's lovely and this place is so beautiful.' Her eyes swept around the cosy room where every table was occupied. 'They're so busy and yet this table wasn't taken. Isn't that strange?'

'Not at all,' he drawled mysteriously. 'This table, with the best view, is always reserved for me.'

Sarah's eyes widened. 'It is? But I didn't see a reservation plaque on it.'

'There never is,' Angus answered with bored arrogance.

'You mean they just keep it for you whether you show up or not?' Sarah asked incredulously.

'That's right.' He smiled across at her,

enjoying her look of astonishment. 'Isn't that nice of them?'

'It's downright stupid!' she blurted, leaning across the table, her green eyes narrowed suspiciously. 'I bet you've got something on the owner, that he's terrified of you and that you're blackmailing him!'

A low chuckle rose from his throat, died abruptly and he shook his head in mock sadness. 'Can't you believe that they're nice to me simply because I'm such a terrific guy?'

The corners of Sarah's mouth twitched and laughter danced in her eyes. 'Sorry,' she said lightly, 'but at the risk of offending your modest ego I would say that something much bigger is involved here. They wouldn't turn away business unless you had something on them.'

'You're right,' Angus sighed, both of them glancing at the queue at the door which they had marched past. 'You're too smart for me.' He leaned towards her, beckoning for her to come closer and Sarah dutifully obeyed. He parted her hair from her ear and whispered into it. 'I own this place! They *have* to be nice to me!' His mouth nuzzled the lobe of her ear and she felt his teeth biting gently into the soft flesh. Desire rose within her, while waves of piercingly beautiful sensations whipped through her. Slowly her head turned and only a feather separated their mouths. Sarah had stopped breathing; she felt suspended in time. Her lips were parted, waiting ... waiting ...

She felt rather than saw Angus move away from her. Her eyes flew open and she saw the mocking cruelty lingering in his own. 'This is such a romantic place,' he said coldly, his voice bordering on harshness, 'that I quite forgot with whom I was sitting. Would you believe I almost kissed you, that I had a burning desire to do so? Now, why would I want to do that to someone who has only the darkest thoughts concerning my character!'

His words hit her like blows. She was still leaning halfway across the table while he was well back in his chair peering down his long arrogant nose at her like a master with a grovelling slave. Her cheeks flamed with colour and her eyes blazed with humiliation. Quickly she sat back, managing to knock over her glass of champagne in the process. She watched in horror as the frothy liquid oozed across the thick linen cloth before finally soaking into the material.

With all the patience of a father accustomed to his unruly child, Angus mopped up the champagne with his napkin while the waiter changed their tablecloth and reset the table. Sarah sat miserably in her chair watching the whole operation, occasionally apologising for her clumsiness which fell on deaf ears, although the waiter did manage a sympathetic smile or two, discreetly taking his cue from the owner of the restaurant.

'I've never been so humiliated in my life!' Sarah said crossly when the waiter had finally finished and moved away. 'You deliberately treated me like a child. How could you do such a thing?'

'Who spilt the champagne?' he growled. 'You or me?'

'I did, but it was your fault!'

'Naturally.'

'Well, it was!' she spat, fresh colour staining her cheeks.

'Because you thought I was going to kiss you and I didn't?' he asked, black eyes rounded in innocence.

'I hate you!' she snarled, sparks flashing from her eyes and her nails biting into the palms of her hands as they itched to slap him, to wipe that smug arrogance from his handsome features.

'Hate me later,' he advised cheerfully, leaning slightly to one side as the waiter placed their orders on the table. He flashed her a smile. 'Calm down. You'll give yourself indigestion.'

Still fuming, Sarah watched in a state of helpless perplexity as Angus cut into the thick rump steak still sizzling on the steel platter it had been served on. In front of her was the *filet mignon* she had ordered, topped with crispy mushrooms and wrapped in bacon. Sighing heavily, Sarah picked up her fork and listlessly popped a mushroom into her mouth. Her taste buds came to life.

'Well, what do you think of my restaurant?' Angus asked when they had finished with the main course and had started on the cheese and fruit platter. 'Does it pass inspection?'

The food, the service, the decor, the clientele and the location on the river bank were top class as Angus had meant them to be. Sarah knew him well enough by now to know that Angus Sawyer never did things by halves. The restaurant didn't need to pass her inspection. It was enough that it had passed his own. His male ego wanted flattery, and Sarah had no doubt he had brought to this place many young women who had filled his ears with what he wanted to hear. Well, he was in for a surprise!

'I'm sure it will be very nice when it's finished,' she said helpfully, smiling demurely across at him, savouring the look of shocked surprise on his disgustingly handsome face.

'*Finished*?' he boomed. 'It *is* finished!'

Her fine brows arched in surprise. 'Oh, really? I would have thought you planned to add a balcony. Something nice and open to look on to the river.'

'A balcony?' His black brows drew together consideringly.

'Yes. You could have tables out there where people could enjoy a pre-dinner drink while they're waiting for their meal to be served.' She sipped at her champagne and smiled sweetly across at him over the rim of her glass. 'I'm amazed you never thought of that yourself.'

Her suggestion, while a good one, she allowed herself to concede, was meant to goad him, to

dampen his ego a little. To her astonishment, he
agreed to it.

'I like it!' He turned in his chair to face the
long row of windows looking out on to the river.
'Those could be removed and replaced with
sliding doors,' he said, turning back to her. 'I'll
get a builder started on it right away. Any other
suggestions?'

'Well-l-l-l, a barbecue might be nice. You
could have a servery on your balcony and people
could eat out there. On Sunday afternoons you
could have a *smorgasbord*.'

His teeth flashed white as he grinned at her.
'The suggestions keep coming forth, don't
they?'

'Well, you did ask!'

'I did indeed, and I like them. Except for
maybe the barbecue. It might make the place too
informal. What do you think?'

'You could be right,' she agreed, finding
herself becoming involved with the changes and
actually enjoying sharing this with him. 'There's
such a lovely feeling of intimacy already. We
wouldn't want to do anything to spoil that.'

He smiled at her serious use of the pronoun.
'No, we wouldn't.' His smile deepened. 'Should
I add a dance-floor? There's plenty of room.'

A dance-floor. A place where he could hold her
in his arms without complications. She could
almost feel what it would be like. Cheek to cheek,
heart to pounding heart.

'Do you enjoy dancing?' she asked, a trifle breathlessly.

'Love it. Don't you?' A warm passion had entered his eyes, and Sarah hastily looked away.

Of course he would love dancing. He would love anything which provided an excuse to get a woman in his arms. *Any* woman! Sarah pressed her back into the chair.

'Dancing is all right,' she conceded reluctantly. She reached for her handbag and pushed away from the table. 'Do you mind if we go now? It's awfully late.'

He ignored her anxious plea. 'In a few minutes.' He spoke roughly. 'Why must you always find excuses to get away from me?'

'I don't! It's just that I'm tired. I've had a long day.'

He looked her fully in the face and sighed. 'Forgive me for my selfishness. You do look tired.' He got up and helped her from her chair, his hands warm on her shoulders.

'But what about the dance-floor?' His breath stirred her hair and caressed the delicate skin of her nape. She half turned to look up at him, shivering at the enigmatic gleam in his eyes.

'It's your restaurant,' she snapped, moving deftly away from him, uncomfortably aware that her angry reaction was in response to her own weakness. How long would it be before he guessed her true feelings? she couldn't help but wonder. She shivered again, but this time from fear. If only she hadn't allowed herself to fall for him.

He steered her out of the restaurant, his arm draped around her shoulders, holding her closer than she thought proper. Once outside, she shrugged out of his grip.

'I'm quite capable of walking on my own,' she said huffily.

Anger flared briefly in his eyes but he said nothing until they were seated in the car. 'I always seem to do and say the wrong things to you, Sarah,' he said, gently turning her face towards him. 'I don't meant to.'

Sarah stared helplessly into his eyes. She was a country girl, homespun and honest. She had never learned to deceive anyone. She had been taught to be open about her feelings, to be truthful in her dealings with others.

She loved Angus. How simple it would be to tell him of her feelings, but she knew she never could. For her own safety and future happiness she must keep her secret forever buried in her heart. She must never allow her feelings for this man to interfere with what she knew was right and decent. Angus Sawyer didn't believe in love and marriage. She did!

'What is it, Sarah?' he asked softly when she didn't answer. She shook her head, the lump in her throat quite preventing any speech. He sighed mournfully. 'Whenever I think I'm getting closer to you, you quite suddenly blot me out, slam the door in my face.' He dragged a rueful hand through his hair. 'Do you really dislike me so much?'

If only he knew! When she still didn't answer he turned abruptly away from her and started the car. The heavy silence was suffocating, and when they pulled up to her flat she opened the car door with hasty relief, something he was quick to notice.

'Escape at last!' he drawled sardonically, and she heard the bitterness in his voice. She was almost out of the car when his hand lashed out and he pulled her back. They stared into each other's eyes. Sarah's heart thrashed madly in her chest and her lips parted. A half-sob tore from her throat as his mouth descended and captured hers.

She melted against him. Her body seemed to flow and blend with his. Her arms went around his neck, her fingers trailing through his thick wiry hair. She felt his hands on her breasts, his mouth leaving hers to burn a trail of fiery kisses down to the hollow of her neck.

'Sarah!' he groaned, burying his head in her shoulder. 'I've got to have you. You're driving me insane!' He raised his head to look at her, his eyes tortured and very black. 'You want me too,' he insisted hoarsely. 'Admit it!'

'N-no, you're wrong,' she choked at last, placing her hands on his chest in a feeble effort to push him away. She winced at the angry frustration which filled his face and then, just as she thought he would release her, his hands gripped her shoulder, jerking her towards him. His mouth ground down on hers in a savage embrace, devouring her, draining away her strength.

Terrified, Sarah fought to free herself, pushing and pummelling at him with her fists. But his superior strength was too much for her, and her traitorous body yielded to the intimacy of his hands. She felt as if her whole body had opened to him, that it no longer belonged to her. Her defences were finally destroyed. Just when she thought there was no turning back, she heard his agonised groan of torment as he broke away from her.

'*Go!*' he commanded savagely, reaching across to swing open the car door.

Sarah swallowed convulsively, her eyes wide and uncomprehending. 'G-go?' she repeated dumbly.

'Yes,' he said flatly, the fire dying in his eyes. 'Go!'

Sarah stumbled from the car and raced up the path to her flat. She could feel his eyes on her even after she was safely inside with the door locked. In her bedroom mirror she stared at herself, hardly believing the wild-eyed, tousled-haired creature was herself. Hysteria rose in her throat at the sight of her rumpled clothing, the small tear in her dress. One earring was missing and her lips were swollen from his kisses.

Shaking violently, Sarah made her way to the telephone. She felt an urgent need to talk to her mother. She picked up the receiver and started dialling, but replaced it again before the call was through. There was no one to turn to, no one who would understand her love for Angus.

She thought of her father. He had been a quiet, unassuming man, a man who had placed gentle kisses on his wife's cheek. Sarah placed trembling fingers to her throbbing lips. Her mother would definitely not understand!

CHAPTER SEVEN

KIRSTEN was waiting for her when she got to work the next morning. Sarah took one look at the frosty blue eyes and knew there was trouble. Kirsten had planted herself in front of Sarah's coat cupboard. Sarah stood in front of her, her pale blue cardigan dangling from her fingers as she waited for Kirsten to step aside so that she might hang it up.

But Kirsten had no intention of moving. She looked coldly into Sarah's clear green eyes. Her lips barely moved as she spoke.

'So,' she hissed. 'You told Angus I *made* you stay back last night to type up the sales reports.'

Sarah frowned. 'I said no such thing.'

'Then why is he so angry?' She switched on the video. 'Look!'

Sarah stared at the small screen. Angus was on the warpath. His hair was mussed and his shirt sleeves were rolled up while his tie hung loosely around his neck. She didn't need the audio to know he was shouting. He had gathered several employees in front of him, and with each point made slammed a huge fist into the palm of his hand. Sarah switched off the machine and sighed. Angus Sawyer had changed into a wild-eyed demon, and she knew she was to blame.

'I've already received my blast!' Kirsten told her. 'He was waiting for me when I got to work.'

Sarah sat down and placed her hands on the surface of the highly polished desk. She looked helplessly up at Kirsten. 'What did he say to you?'

'He *said* I wasn't treating you fairly. He *said* I was giving you too much work. He *said* I was to increase your pay, make it equal to *mine*!' She leaned towards Sarah. 'I knew you were trouble the moment I laid eyes on you. You're after my job!'

'Listen, Kirsten,' Sarah said wearily. 'Angus might have been a bit upset to find me working so late but ...'

'So late!' Kirsten interrupted. 'What time did you finish those figures?' she demanded to know.

Sarah shrugged. 'Around eight but ...'

'Eight o'clock!' Her blue eyes narrowed. 'You were *waiting* for him! Oh, don't deny it. You should have finished before eight. You must have known Angus would be dropping around to examine the displays for the junior social club.'

'I didn't, I ...'

'Oh, don't think I haven't noticed the way you look at him,' Kirsten continued, her voice rising shrilly. 'Those big green eyes of yours following his every move whenever he's here. You must have found out somehow that he would be here last night. No wonder you so willingly agreed to stay back and do those reports,' she declared triumphantly.

'May I remind you, Kirsten, that I've quite willingly stayed back on several other occasions without running into Angus. Why should this time be different?'

'But it was different, wasn't it? This time you got lucky!'

'Don't be ridiculous!'

Kirsten laughed softly. 'You've got it bad, real bad. You're really hooked on the guy.' She laughed again. 'You and a thousand others!'

Sarah looked at her calmly. 'And what about you, Kirsten?' she asked. 'Are you one of the thousand?'

Kirsten eyed her shrewdly. 'What do you think?'

'I think . . . I know Angus thinks very highly of you,' Sarah replied slowly. 'You . . . you've been working together for a . . . a long time.'

'And that gives me the edge over you, doesn't it, little Miss Sarah Ames?' She looked down her nose at Sarah and smiled maliciously. 'One day Angus will realise he needs a wife to provide him with an heir. I fully intend to be the woman he chooses.'

Sarah looked at Kirsten with pity in her eyes. Angus would never belong to anyone other than himself, and gradually over the years Kirsten had come to realise this. Her only hope now was the possibility of Angus wanting a child to reap the benefits of his huge fortune. She shook her head sadly.

'But what kind of life would you have,

Kirsten?' she asked softly. 'Even if Angus did marry for the reason you mentioned, do you think he could be content with just one woman? He ... he's a womaniser. You must realise that. He would break your heart. Lots of money and lots of women. Money and women, women and money. How could you possibly wish to spend the rest of your life with a man like *that*?'

Kirsten's laugh was filled with a ruthless contempt. 'Who are you trying to convince? Me or yourself?' She laughed again at the sight of Sarah's fiery red cheeks. 'Haven't you heard of divorce settlements? I'm no fool, you know. I might never possess his heart but I fully intend to share in his wealth.' She added bitterly, 'I deserve *something*!'

Sarah looked at Kirsten's cold, unhappy face and shivered.

The door opened and both women turned to find Angus glaring in at them. His expression was dark and brooding but it in no way detracted from his good looks. A tweed jacket was slung carelessly across one broad shoulder.

'Having a hen party are we, ladies?' he snapped, stepping into the office and slamming the door behind him. His glare singled out Kirsten. 'While you've been in here gossiping your telephone has been ringing.'

'I ... I was just getting the sales reports,' Kirsten managed nervously. 'You ... you did say to fetch them.'

Angus made a point of looking at his watch.

'That was twenty minutes ago. Why aren't they on my desk?'

Sarah jumped up and unlocked her filing cabinet, avoiding Angus's eyes as she quickly handed them to Kirsten. Kirsten grabbed the reports and hurriedly left the office. Angus shut the door after her and turned to Sarah.

'How are you this morning?' he asked quietly.

'I'm fine, thank you,' she answered, a trifle breathlessly, flicking back the wavy mane of hair which fell softly across her shoulders before sitting down at her desk. 'But what about you?' she smiled, but there was anxiety in her eyes. 'A bit grouchy, aren't you?'

'Grouchy?' He dragged a rueful hand through his hair. 'That's putting it mildly. I'm in a raging black mood!' He came and sat on the edge of her desk, staring at her so intently that she lowered her eyes in confusion. 'You know what's wrong with me, don't you, Sarah?' and she looked up quickly at the almost pleading tone in his voice.

'I . . . I . . .' She shook her head helplessly. 'No, I'm sorry but I don't.'

'You're lying!' He reached across and cupped her chin, forcing her to look straight into his tortured eyes.

'I want to make love to you, Sarah,' he said in a choking voice. 'I've never wanted another woman the way I want you.' He shook his dark head as though he couldn't quite believe what he was admitting. 'In my mind I've made love to you a thousand times in a thousand different ways. I'm obsessed with you, dammit!'

Sarah put her hand up to touch his and the contact was electrifying. She snatched her hand away and jumped up from her chair.

'You're too used to getting everything you want, Angus,' she said in a trembling voice. 'If ... if you ... if we made love you would be satisfied, wouldn't you? That's all you want. Your ego is suffering because I've said no. You can't understand that some women want to save themselves for their husbands, that marriage comes first.'

He stared at her. 'Save themselves for their husbands?' he asked incredulously.

'That's right,' Sarah replied stiffly, tilting her chin defiantly.

'You're a virgin,' he stated flatly. 'I'm not surprised. I rather suspected you might be.' He looked wonderingly at her. 'I didn't think such creatures still existed.'

Colour flooded her cheeks.

She couldn't believe she was discussing such a personal matter with a self-professed rogue.

'Not all of us live for the moment,' she answered shyly, feeling his eyes penetrating through to her very soul. 'Some of us have the courage of our convictions and find it easy to say no to free love.'

'And do you think I live for the moment?' he asked her quietly.

'Yes, I do. At least as far as ... as sex is concerned.'

He got up and circled her desk, placing his hands on her shoulders. 'But with us it would be different. You could move in with me. You've seen my house, how big it is. I could make life easy for you. You wouldn't have to work.'

'I find your suggestion just as distasteful now as I did when you put it to me before, Angus Sawyer,' she said haughtily, glaring up at him. 'When are you going to get it through your thick head that I am my own person. I will not be compromised!'

He sighed heavily and dropped his hands, leaning down to press his forehead against hers. 'You could have your own bedroom. Think of the money you would save.'

'You really are incorrigible!'

'I know, but I can't help myself.' He kissed the tip of her nose. 'Please say yes.'

She smiled up at him. She really couldn't stay angry for long. How could any woman resist him? Her smile deepened when she saw that he thought she was weakening. He obviously decided his persistence had paid off, that she had been a little harder to persuade than most others but persuade her he had. Sarah peeped up at him through her long silky lashes.

'My own bedroom, eh?'

'The very best in the house,' he agreed, adding enthusiastically, 'You can choose your own.'

'And you would provide me with three good meals a day?'

'Only the finest foods and wines would be

placed before you. Every meal would be a feast.'

'And you said I wouldn't have to work? That you would make life easy for me?' she asked in a wide-eyed wonder.

'That's right,' he drawled, black eyes gleaming.

'It sounds almost too good to be true,' she mused a little doubtfully.

'And I'll buy you a car,' he added quickly.

Her eyes widened. 'A car, too?'

He nodded. 'I can see you in a Mercedes sports sedan.'

'Oh, I don't know, Angus,' she sighed, turning away to stand before the picture windows. 'I'm so used to being on my own, having my own money to spend.'

He came to stand behind her, his hands burning her shoulders, gently caressing her already fevered flesh.

'But of course I'll be giving you an allowance,' he drawled huskily against her ear, his warm breath stirring the soft hairs on the nape of her neck. 'Double what I'm paying you here.'

She whirled to face him, her face animated with delight.

'Oh, Angus!' she breathed, eyes shining. 'I accept!' She stood on her toes and reached up to drag his face down to hers, kissing him warmly on the mouth. 'Mother will be so pleased. I'll be the first in the family to get married!'

'*Married!*'

She almost laughed aloud at the genuine

horror on his face, the shock in his eyes.

'But of course!' She smiled impishly and hit him playfully on the arm. 'And you're so *rich*! Who would have thought little Sarah Ames would land such a prize!' She danced around him. 'My own Mercedes sports sedan!'

He grabbed her wrists and pulled her aginst his hard chest and she could feel the racing beat of his heart. She sincerely hoped he wouldn't have a seizure.

'I never said anything about *marriage*!'

Her mouth dropped open and her eyes widened in surprise. 'But of course you did!'

'I most certainly did not!' The words were clipped and emphatically spaced.

'But . . . but I would be living with you, eating your food, spending your money, driving the car you bought for me. Doesn't that mean I would be your *wife*?'

'It certainly does not!'

Her eyes clouded in confusion. 'But . . . but what *does* it mean?' Suddenly she drew her hands up to her mouth and pressed her knuckles to her lips, green eyes widening in mock horror. 'Oh, Angus!' she gasped. 'You wanted me to be your *mistress*!'

He had the grace to look uncomfortable. 'I detest that term.'

'So do I. It sounds so *used*!' She was angry now, seethingly so. 'How dare you think I can be bought? A Mercedes sports sedan indeed! Do

you usually offer such extravagant gifts to your
. . . women?'

'You're the first. Usually I'm enough.'

She glared up at him. 'I should take you up on
your offer, take everything and give you nothing.
It could be done you know. I would lock my
bedroom door at night and not let you anywhere
near me. You would soon learn that not
everything can be bought.'

'All right, Sarah,' he said tiredly, rubbing his
hand across his jaw. 'You've had your bit of fun,
taken your pound of flesh and managed to make a
prize fool of me in the process.' He scowled down
at her. 'Did you really think I was proposing
marriage?'

She couldn't resist digging her heels in a little
farther. 'Do chickens have teeth?'

Black brows drew together in a frown. 'Marriage,' he said, the word sounding like a shudder
as it passed from his lips. 'You must know I
would make a lousy husband.'

'Probably,' she answered, pretending noncha-
lance as she tugged at a small thread on the
waistband of her blue plaid skirt.

'You don't give me much credit for anything,
do you?' he snapped angrily.

She looked up in surprise. '*You* said you would
make a lousy husband. Those were your words,
not mine.'

'But you agreed.'

She smiled sweetly. 'I like to be agreeable
sometimes.'

His eyes darkened. 'Why do I bother with you?'

She looked at him with honesty in her eyes. 'Because you consider me a challenge. You can't stand having me refuse your lucrative offers. You're not in the least interested in Sarah Ames the person. You're only interested in her body!'

An angry flush crept across the hard lines of his face. 'You're such a smug little thing!' He drew in a deep breath and let it out slowly. 'You place too much importance on sex.'

She had to laugh. '*I* do?'

'Of course,' he grimly agreed. 'If all I was after was a romp in bed I could have that with anyone.'

'Like Pat, Rhonda, Joan, Cynthia, Katie, Kym, Kellie?' she asked jerkily, tears shimmering in her almond-shaped eyes. 'I read the newspapers, you know. I've heard all about your little adventures.'

Tears glistened like tiny jewels on her lashes and he stared down at them in wide-eyed wonder. 'You're crying,' he said huskily, reaching to touch them.

Sarah brushed his hand away and swiped madly at the treacherous things. 'I'm not crying,' she insisted miserably. 'It's just that you make me so . . . angry!'

He drew a ragged breath. 'All right. We'll leave it for now.' He glanced at his watch and sighed. 'I've got that damned meeting to attend.'

She reached up and straightened his tie. Her

hands were so pale next to the tanned column of his throat.

'Yes,' she agreed chokingly, her fingers lingering on his tie. He reached up and clasped his hands around hers and black eyes locked to green. Slowly he raised her hands to press them against his mouth. Sarah swayed against him, losing herself in the dizzying vortex of those enigmatic black pools.

'You pretend not to like me, Sarah,' he whispered softly, 'yet I know you must.'

'No,' she protested weakly, but even as she uttered the denial she could see the disbelieving lights in his eyes.

'You cared enough to fix my tie,' he murmured quietly. 'You wouldn't have done that if you didn't care.'

The words were spoken so seriously that Sarah had to smile. There was a lot of the little boy left in the man. She adjusted the tie a little more. 'I used to do this for my father,' she explained. 'He never could get it right. Then I taught my little brother.'

'So it's nothing more than habit, is that what you're telling me?' he enunciated slowly, disappointment clouding his eyes.

Sarah swallowed hard, then smiled brightly, 'It must be.'

He nodded and dropped her hands, stuffing his own into his trouser pockets. Immediately he withdrew one hand, looked silently at what he held and then placed the earring in her palm.

'I found it in my car,' he said. 'It's yours, isn't it?'

Her fingers closed around the little bauble. 'Yes, thank you.' Two hot spots of colour appeared high on her cheeks. 'I guess it must be hard keeping track of what women leave behind in your car.'

He jerked himself erect. 'It doesn't happen as often as you might think,' he replied stiffly. He seemed about to say more but obviously thought better of it. Glowering darkly, he turned and left her office. At noon she saw him leave the plant. Instinct told her he wouldn't be back.

By the end of the day Sarah felt wrung out in more ways than one. The day had been particularly busy, the work demanding, and made more so by hoping Angus would ring or call back at the plant for her.

At her flat, Sarah prepared a meal she didn't feel like eating, then sat at the kitchen table working on her assignments. At nine-thirty she closed her books and stared vacantly at the walls of the tiny kitchen. Loneliness washed over her in mounting waves. She knew she would give anything to spend the rest of her life with Angus, and she wondered how many other women had felt the same.

Her eyes drifted back to her books. What had she worked on the whole evening? She couldn't remember. It was as if he had taken over her mind, crowding out everything except the sound of his voice, the flashing of his coal-black eyes which crinkled at the corners when he laughed, the feel of his hands on her body, the thrill of his lips on hers. She was completely and totally intoxicated by him, and for this there was no cure. Sighing heavily, Sarah finally got up and prepared for bed. When she stepped from the shower, she was startled to hear the doorbell ringing. She slipped into her bathrobe, tying the belt around her slender waist as she hurried to answer the persistent ring.

'Who is it?' she demanded through the wooden structure.

'Angus. May I come in or shall I blow the door down?' was the gruff reply.

Sarah opened the door immediately, unable to conceal her delight at this unexpected treat.

'Angus!' she breathed happily, stepping aside so he could enter. 'This *is* a surprise!'

His eyes trailed over her, taking in the scruffy pink robe, the shining face and eyes, the damp tendrils of hair clinging to her rosy cheeks. Her feet were bare, the dainty ankles peeking provocatively below the hem of the robe. He smiled warmly down at her, black brows raised in surprise that she should greet him so enthusiastically. Heartened by this, his arms swept around her and he was holding her close, his lips nuzzling the clean fragrant hair as she pressed her cheek to his chest, her own arms around him as if they hadn't seen one another for years.

'I'm here on business,' he drawled huskily,

holding her away from him so he could watch her face.

'Oh? What is it?' she asked, snuggling into the warm enclosure of his arms once more. He picked her up and carried her into the lounge, sitting down with her on his lap in one of the chairs.

His eyes seemed to devour her face as she waited for him to tell her. His hand circled her neck and then his lips were on hers and she returned the kiss with an urgency which matched his. She felt him part her bathrobe and she was both thrilled and terrified. The feel of his hands against her caused her to gasp with exquisite delight.

Warm and caressing, they worked their way down to her waist and across the silky skin of her stomach before he quite abruptly and firmly gathered the folds of her robe and fastened the belt.

'Sarah,' he groaned. 'I'm sorry, I didn't mean that to happen. I didn't *plan* it,' he added heavily, obviously thinking she wouldn't believe him.

'I . . . I know,' Sarah told him, her voice barely a whisper. 'We always seem to end up in each other's arms.'

He knelt in front of her, taking both her hands in his.

'And that's why I'm here,' he said, a desperate quality in his voice as he searched her face. 'I want to prove to you that you're safe with me. I want to prove that I can be with you without making a ... a grab for you. I want you to learn to trust me.'

He was being so earnest that she couldn't help but smile at him. 'And how do you propose to do that?' she asked softly, losing herself as she always did in the black volumes of his eyes.

His hands tightened around hers sending wild shocks up her arms and across to her heart. 'I have business down the coast at Surfers Paradise.' His face broke into a grin, teeth flashing white against his tanned face. 'Have you ever been to Sea World?'

'Why no, never.' Her smooth brow puckered into a frown. 'What have Surfers Paradise and Sea World got to do with me?'

'It's quite simple.' His hands moved up her arms, drawing her closer so that her face was on a level with his own. 'You're coming with me!'

Her clear green eyes widened in astonishment while she was conscious of an excitement burning in the pit of her stomach. 'I am?'

He was clearly pleased with her reaction. 'Yes, it will only be for the day. I'm leaving first thing in the morning. Can you be ready by seven o'clock?'

'Yes but ... but what about my job?'

'Kirsten can handle any emergencies while you're gone.' He kissed the tip of her nose. 'You deserve a break from the place.'

Sarah rose shakily to her feet and he rose with her, his hands still on her arms, her breasts lightly touching the hard wall of his chest. 'I ... I don't know what to say,' she replied breathlessly, desperately trying to ignore the wild clamourings of her naked body beneath the thin robe. To spend a whole day with Angus Sawyer was more than she'd ever dreamed of, and to spend it at Surfers Paradise would make it all the more romantic.

'Say yes!'

Her eyes swept up to his face. 'You . . . you said you were going on business,' she reminded him. 'Is there something you wanted me to help you with?'

'If I said no, would you refuse to come?' He placed his hands on her shoulders and gave her a little shake. 'I'm offering you a day on the coast away from the humdrum of the office. We'll be there and back in one day. That hardly gives me the chance to seduce you.'

Sarah knew he was angry and she realised he had every right to be. She was behaving like a prissy old maid, and the irony of it was that nothing could be further from the truth. A day alone with Angus spelt romance whether it was filled with business or not.

'I'll go,' she said briskly forcing a businesslike tone into her voice. 'I was just thinking about my job, that's all. But as you say, Kirsten is certainly capable of looking after things.'

The hard look in his eyes softened now that she had agreed and the grip on her shoulders relaxed. He ran his hands lightly down her arms. 'Good. Now even though we'll only be gone the day you'll need a couple of changes of clothing.'

Sarah eyed him suspiciously. 'Whatever for?'

'Because it will be hot and we'll be doing a lot of tramping around Sea World. You will want shorts and you will probably want to go for a swim. I have a unit on the beach; you can change there. Eventually you will get hungry and I'll need to feed you. Unless you want a hamburger at a take-away, you'll need something fashionable for a restaurant.' He sighed heavily and shook his head. 'Any more suspicions, or have we covered them all?'

Sarah grinned. She might have known a day with Angus would be three days rolled into one. 'You haven't told me what we shall be doing at Sea World. I hope you won't make me ride the roller-coaster.'

He cupped her face with his hands and kissed her lightly on the lips. 'I would never make you do anything you didn't want to,' he said seriously, 'but I think we will have time for a little fun. Mostly I want to check out the electronic equipment I have there and see what needs replacing.' He put his arms around her and hugged her close. 'Now go to bed and get some rest so you'll be bright and cheerful for me in the morning.' He reluctantly released her. 'I doubt I'll be able to sleep at all.'

But Sarah certainly did. In fact she slept extremely well. She dreamt of him, and when she woke in the morning there was a smile on her lips.

CHAPTER EIGHT

SARAH glanced at Angus. What was he thinking? she wondered. Judging from the look on his face, she decided his thoughts must be extremely pleasant. He turned his attention from the road and smiled down at her, one hand leaving the steering-wheel to cover hers folded on her lap.

Sarah returned his smile, and when he took his hand away to place it again on the steering-wheel she turned towards the window, staring unseeingly at the passing scenery as they sped towards Surfers Paradise. She wondered what the day would bring. Angus had said it would be strictly business and she believed him. What frightened her was herself. She loved him so. She wanted, needed to be as close to him as only two people in love could be.

And that was the problem. How could she keep her secret hidden when she would be in his company for a whole day. She wasn't superwoman, for goodness sake!

He had arrived earlier than expected, but even so she was ready and waiting with one small suitcase already packed. She had been watching the street below, and when the red Maserati had pulled up outside her flat her heart had jumped crazily all over her chest and her mouth and throat had gone suddenly dry. When the doorbell rang she jumped as if from shock, and it was several seconds before she was able to pull across the latch to let him in. And when she did every pulse in her body leapt at the sight of him.

He was dressed in cream-coloured slacks, a short-sleeved black silk shirt opened at the neck. He looked alarmingly virile, totally male. His smile swept over her and she felt her insides turn to jelly. Dear God, she prayed, save me from myself and my own wicked desires!

He stepped inside and kissed her cheek. She had offered her lips but he chose her cheek and she knew why. He was letting her know that he could content himself with this slight show of affection. What he didn't know was that even something so casual as a kiss on the cheek sparked fire in her veins.

'You look lovely, Sarah,' he said huskily, and she bowed her head in sudden shyness, thrilled beyond belief at the simple compliment.

She hadn't known what to wear. What does one wear when one embarks on a day-long journey with the man one secretly loves? she had wondered. She had finally chosen a plain white frock, sleeveless, with a red belt tucked around her slender waist. Her only make-up was a touch of gloss on her lips and she had pulled her hair back, securing the shining chestnut-coloured wings with tortoiseshell clips. She looked young and vulnerable. Only the red belt at her waist hinted that her thoughts might not be as innocent as her appearance.

'Would you like a cup of coffee or something before we leave?' she had asked breathlessly, this feeling of shyness growing in intensity.

'No, thanks. I'd like to get away as soon as possible,' he had answered, his voice low as he watched her. 'Are you looking forward to the day?'

Her eyes had sparkled with delight. 'Oh yes, very much so.' Did she have to sound so eager?

He had smiled. 'Good, but you seem a little edgy. There's nothing wrong, I hope?'

She had laughed then, a nervous, twittery sound even to her own ears. 'I guess I just can't help thinking how fortunate I am to have such a wonderful job.'

'*And* a wonderful boss?'

She had laughed again. 'Yes, that too. I feel . . . important. My family will be very impressed to learn that my job takes me away on business. They'll think I run the place.'

He had chuckled and put his arm around her shoulders. 'Well, I have asked you to be a partner on a number of occasions,' he had said teasingly.

She had ducked from under his arm. 'Well, I will be today.'

'I didn't mean *business* partner,' he had said softly, not letting her off so easily.

She had looked him straight in the eye. '*I* did, and if you've got any tricks up your sleeve . . .'

He had silenced her with an impatient wave of

his hand. 'I was merely joking, but if this trip is going to upset you in any way then there's really no point in you coming.'

Panic had seized her. 'Oh no,' she had quickly answered. 'I want to go.' Good grief! she had thought, I'm *pleading* with him! If I'm like this now what will I be like when he no longer has any interest in me? A picture of Kirsten flashed through her mind and she shuddered. Would her own features become hard and brittle, her eyes like cold green chips?

'Then let's be on our way.' He had picked up her small suitcase and tested it for weight. 'You're a light packer,' he had said approvingly. 'Usually women think it's necessary to bring their whole wardrobe.'

'I *did* bring my whole wardrobe!' And this time when she laughed it was a rich, merry sound and he had joined her, their laughter washing away their tensions. It was going to be a good day, a great day, a day she hoped she would treasure for the rest of her life.

And now here they were practically at Surfers Paradise and with each passing kilometre her excitement increased. She wondered what his unit would be like, what they would talk about, what they would do at Sea World, where they would go to dine.

'What's your unit like?' she asked without looking his way. 'Is it big?'

'Quite big,' he agreed.

Several more kilometres went by before she

spoke again. 'How many bedrooms does it have?'

'Four, each with a view of the ocean.'

'Is it right on the beach?'

'Any closer and you would be in the water.'

'It sounds nice.'

'And you sound a trifle apprehensive.'

'I am a little,' she admitted with a sigh. 'I can't help feeling I'm playing truant, both from my studies and my job. I have a lecture tonight at eight. Do you think we'll be back by then?'

'Not a chance,' he answered without a shred of remorse in his voice. 'The world won't come to an end if you miss just one lecture.'

'I know, but it spoils my perfect record. I haven't missed a single lecture since I started the course, nor have I missed a day's work. Not bad, eh?'

He shot her a grin. 'Perfection from every pore.'

She laughed. 'Not perfect maybe, but pretty close to it. Even when I'm sick I go to work and lectures.' She pressed her back into the soft cushion and sighed happily. 'I guess I do deserve this little break.'

'You deserve a Caribbean cruise,' he declared solemnly, and she laughed, thoroughly enjoying his company.

'Anyway, your work record is still intact,' Angus told her a few minutes later. 'Officially, this is a business trip.'

'I brought a notebook and pencils,' Sarah told him. 'I didn't know what else to bring. I should have asked.' She looked anxiously up at him.

'A notebook and pencils are fine, just fine,' he assured her, placing his hand on her knee. 'Had I wanted anything in particular I would have told you.'

Sarah didn't answer. She was staring down at his huge tanned hand caressing her knee, frighteningly aware of the excited shivers coursing through her body. She knew she must remove his hand, but when she went to do so he merely grabbed it and raised it to his lips.

'Look ahead, Sarah,' he murmured against her trembling fingers. 'There's Surfers.'

Surfers Paradise loomed ahead in all its glory. Sparkling blue waters washed the white sandy shores while stately green palm trees swayed in the soft breezes. Modern apartment buildings towered above the causeway, stretching into the cloudless blue skies. Tourists and locals decked out in scanty tropical gear strolled leisurely along the green leafy streets. Bicycles built for two, motorised carts, mini-mokes and quaint little cars zipped through the slow-moving traffic. Sarah's excitement grew as she soaked up the atmosphere. Surfers Paradise! What a name ... what a *place*!

Angus drew up to a sparkling white building surrounded by beautifully landscaped gardens. Sarah's eyes danced over the array of hibiscus shrubs ranging in colour from whites to the deepest pinks and corals. Dark green leaves formed backdrops to waterfalls and cascades of yellow and white bell-shaped blossoms. Palms rustled and swayed and next to them sprawled the branches of frangipani trees, their delightful waxy blossoms filling the air with sweet tropical scent. It truly was a paradise, and it was hers for a day. She leaned against the deep leather uphol-stery, her hair fanning the headrest, and let out a long, contented sigh.

'I can't believe I'm here,' she said softly. 'It's everything I always heard it was, even more.'

Angus leaned towards her, his fingers splaying through the russet strands of her hair. 'You haven't been to Surfers before now?'

'No, this is my first time,' she answered breathlessly, caught in the mystic aura of those incredibly black eyes.

'Then I'm honoured to be the one to show you around.' His mouth was dangerously close to hers. 'Glad you came?'

'Yes,' she breathed, completely intoxicated by his closeness and by his hand stroking her hair. Her nostrils quivered with the clean male scent of him, a heady sensation, and she was aware of her body leaning towards his, drawn against him as by a magnetic force which she was powerless to resist. There was a roaring in her ears louder than the pounding of the nearby surf and she thought that he must surely hear it too. He was so close, so agonisingly close ...

'Angus,' she groaned. Her hand went up to his cheek, her fingers lovingly tracing the strong line of his jaw and the hard handsome curve of his mouth. He caught her pink-tipped finger and closed his teeth around it. The sharp pain was exquisite, sending fresh shock waves through her system. He drew the finger deeper into his mouth, his eyes burning with desire as he watched the effect this was having on her.

Suddenly he drew away. 'Come on, Sarah,' he said in a gruff-sounding voice, his head turning away from her as he spoke. 'I'll take you up to the penthouse. We'll have breakfast there.'

He got out of the car and walked around to help her out. His manner was so grim that she dared not speak. She felt as though he had somehow rejected her, and the brilliant sun burned painfully on her suddenly frozen skin. She hugged her arms against her chest and shivered. An attendant came for the car and drove it down to an underground car park. Angus took her arm and led her up to the building and through the lavishly decorated foyer towards the lifts. Neither spoke as they were being transported up to the penthouse.

Angus gave her a brief tour of the unit, thereby introducing her to another world. No expense had been spared. The décor was exquisite down to the smallest detail. Each of the four bedrooms had its own bathroom and private balcony with sweeping views of the ocean. The dining-room could easily cater for twenty or more people and the lounge was enormous, stretching the full length of the dwelling and spilling on to the tiled patio with its panoramic views of Surfers

Paradise, the ocean, the canals and the streets below.

There was a heated swimming-pool, spa and sauna. Lounging chairs and tables were protected from the sun with bright green-and-white-striped umbrellas. Shrubs and potted palms completed the picture. Sarah stood in the midst of all this and shook her head in wonder. Angus had his own private paradise right here in this penthouse. If only her family could see her now ...!

Angus picked up her bag and Sarah followed him into one of the huge bedrooms decorated in pale shades of pink. She felt like Alice in Wonderland and that any minute she would awaken from this fantastic dream.

Angus glanced at his watch. 'I'll ring down for some breakfast,' he said, maintaining his formal attitude as though this might be the only defence he had against her.

'Ring down for breakfast?' she repeated in surprise. 'You mean there's a restaurant in the building?'

'Several, as a matter of fact. What would you like? Bacon and eggs? Ham and eggs? An omelette?'

Sarah didn't answer. Instead she sat down on the huge four-poster bed. The bed was so high that her feet didn't touch the floor and she swung her legs back and forth. 'This is fun,' she announced gaily, unable to resist bouncing on the springy mattress.

Angus watched her in amused silence, only the small muscle twitching alongside his hard jaw hinting at the remarkable restraint he was showing by not joining her on the bed.

'Sarah,' he growled at last. 'Stop fooling around and tell me what you want for breakfast. You can have anything you want. Sausages and eggs . . .'

She gave one final bounce and jumped off the bed. 'Do they have pancakes?' she asked eagerly.

He smiled at her, his eyes resting on the shimmering halo of her reddish-brown hair before slipping down to the eager expectation in her eyes.

'I think so. How do you like them? With lemon and sugar?'

She shook her head. 'No, with maple syrup.' She laughed almost shamefully. 'Surrounded in all this luxury, I feel I can make any demand I wish and that it will be granted.'

'Queen for a day, hm?'

'And a good thing it is only for a day,' she agreed quite happily, 'or I might become spoilt.' She kicked off her shoes and sighed with pleasure as her feet slowly sank into the soft luxurious pile of the carpet.

A tender longing entered Angus's eyes as he watched her. Then abruptly he turned and walked from the bedroom. Sarah unzipped her bag and removed the lime-green shorts and matching top she would wear to Sea World and the lemon-yellow frock she would wear for dinner. Her bathing-suit was almost the colour of the blue ocean which seemed to beckon from the opened patio. Angus had said there would be time for a swim and while the ocean certainly looked inviting it was hard to ignore the beautifully tiled pool. Perhaps there would be time for both.

Sarah hung her dress in the wall-length wardrobe while her shorts, top, underwear and bathing suit went into a huge chest of drawers. Humming happily, she went to find Angus. He was standing on the tiled patio staring out to sea.

'I'm all unpacked,' she announced. 'Have you ordered breakfast?'

'Yes, it's on the way.' His dark eyes remained fixed on the rolling sea.

Sarah touched his arm. 'Is something wrong, Angus?' she asked quietly.

He turned and saw the anxiety in her eyes and looked pointedly down at her hand. Sarah quickly removed it, feeling a chill closing around her heart. Angus left her to stand alone on the patio with its exquisite view while he lost himself in the penthouse.

She heard the sound of a buzzer and knew breakfast had arrived, but she no longer felt hungry. Angus called her and she reluctantly joined him in the dining-room.

The table had been set for two and in the centre was a huge platter stacked high with pancakes. Beside it was a jug of maple syrup.

Angus was in the process of pouring juice into two glasses and when she entered the room he held out a chair for her. She sat down and spread the snowy white linen napkin across her lap, keeping her eyes lowered. His manner was so brusque and formal that she didn't want to see what was in his eyes. The day had barely started but it seemed it had already lost its charm.

Angus sat across from her and when she felt him watching her she lifted her face and tried desperately to smile but the frozen muscles in her face refused to perform.

He didn't help her. In fact it came to her that he seemed as tense as she was. What had gone wrong? Frantically she searched her mind for a clue and the best she could come up with was the pancakes. Angus had suggested bacon and eggs, but she had insisted upon pancakes and maple syrup. She shouldn't have done that, she ...

'I shouldn't have ordered pancakes,' she blurted. 'I ... I bet you don't like pancakes. I'm sorry, Angus, I ...'

He arched his dark brows in astonishment at her sudden outburst.

'I love them,' he growled.

'You do?'

'Of course. If I didn't I would have ordered something else.'

He placed pancakes on both their plates and when he picked up the jug of syrup Sarah was amazed to see that his hand was shaking.

Finally she understood. There was no blame involved here. Angus Sawyer, the good-time guy, was simply terrified. *Of her!*

He loves me! she thought with a burst of delirious joy.

CHAPTER NINE

SARAH wanted breakfast to last for ever. Never had her man been so attentive nor looked so handsome. He watched her while she ate, hardly eating any himself. Their conversation was pleasant but centred totally on business. Sarah didn't mind. She loved hearing his plans for expansion, and especially his increasing interest in the youth group.

'We've got thirty kids coming to the plant on a regular basis now,' he said. 'And a few have asked if their friends can join.'

Sarah knew he was pleased with this. 'That's wonderful. It proves they must be really enjoying themselves.'

Angus nodded. 'It also proves another thing. There's a growing need for factories like mine to open their doors to children and help them put their time to some constructive use.' He leaned back in his chair and grimaced. 'You'd be surprised at how many of those kids reminded me of myself at that age, although I don't think I was quite as bitter as some.' He smiled suddenly. 'In the weeks we've had the club going there have been miraculous changes in a few of the more, shall we say *aggressive* personalities. Once or twice I came close to calling a halt to the whole

155

project, but I'm glad now I didn't. The worst kids have proved the brightest.'

Sarah agreed. 'In most cases I think their behaviour is directly linked to frustration. They have the ability to go to university but know their families can't afford to send them. Part-time jobs are harder to find and living-costs have risen dramatically. It's now practically impossible to attend university full-time without benefit of a scholarship plus financial support from your family. For some families that can mean real hardship and total sacrifice.'

They had pushed their plates and coffee-cups away and sat with arms folded on the table, heads close together as they continued their discussion. It was only when the porter came to clear away the table that Angus looked at his watch and exclaimed in astonishment. 'Eleven o'clock! We've been talking for over two hours!'

Sarah checked her own watch and found that this was true. Her cheeks were flushed from their debate and her eyes were sparkling. She jumped up from the table. 'I'll get changed. It will only take a minute.'

'I'm feeling generous,' Angus drawled. 'Take three minutes.'

She compromised and was out in two. Angus was on the telephone but when he looked up and saw the vision of loveliness silhouetted against the opened patio door he quickly put an end to his conversation.

'Where do you think you're going dressed like

that?' he demanded to know. His dark eyes trailed slowly over her slender figure, casually dressed in the shorts and top and with white scuffies on her feet.

Her eyes widened in surprise. 'Why, to Sea World . . . with you. You said to wear shorts and a top.'

'When did I say that?'

'Last night. You said it would be more comfortable.'

He frowned darkly. 'That was last night.' He dragged his hand through his hair. 'Put on some slacks.'

'I didn't bring any. Besides slacks would be too hot. This outfit is fine. It's light and you did say you wanted me to be comfortable,' she reminded him cheekily.

'You might be comfortable, but I wouldn't be,' he growled. 'With those legs supporting that figure Sea World would come to a halt!'

She cocked her head and grinned impishly up at him. 'Are you trying to tell me I have beautiful legs and a beautiful figure, Angus Sawyer?'

He placed his hands on her shoulders and spun her in the direction of the bedroom. 'Put on the dress you wore down.' He gave her a little push but it wasn't enough to make her do as she was told. She whirled back to face him.

'I'll put on the dress only after you've answered my question.'

He shoved his hands into his pockets and scowled at her. 'What question?'

'Nothing,' she murmured softly. 'I'll ... I'll go and change.'

'Sarah,' he called after her.

She turned. 'Yes?'

'In answer to your question, you're every inch a beauty!'

Her delighted smile danced across her lovely features. She didn't really care whether she was beautiful or not. It was enough that Angus thought her so. He had complimented her before but this time she knew it was different.

'You're not so bad yourself,' she said, generously returning the compliment. Their eyes met across the room and the world became still. Neither spoke nor did they move. It was Angus who cruelly broke the spell.

'Get changed, Sarah,' he snarled. 'You're wasting my time.'

Her cheeks paled and she swallowed hard. She knew he had felt what had passed between them. How much longer could he go on denying his feelings, she wondered, as tears of despair welled in her eyes.

'I'm sorry you think I'm wasting your time,' she said, frantically blinking back tears. 'But may I remind you, Angus Sawyer, that I *am* ready! You told me to bring shorts and a top.' She stamped her small foot in a gesture of helplessness. 'I try so hard to please you.'

He took several steps towards her but stopped before she was within arm's length. His eyes were as stormy as the black clouds looming unnoticed in the quickly darkening skies. A ferocious clap of thunder shattered the uneasy stillness which had gripped them, and when lightning pierced the atmosphere she felt it in her heart.

'The Devil takes care of its own,' she gasped, as another, louder clap boomed through the heavy atmosphere, causing her to start like a frightened doe.

Angus reached for her but she clasped her arms across her breast and backed away.

'Sarah, please.'

'The heavens have spoken for you, Angus,' she said tearfully, not meaning to sound so dramatic. 'You've got the excuse you've been waiting for.' As she spoke torrential rain began to fall. 'You'll say I can't go now. You'll say you don't want me getting wet.' Her teeth were chattering but it had nothing to do with the cold southerly breezes sweeping through the opened patio doors.

'Don't be ridiculous,' he snarled. 'I didn't create this storm.' He looked towards the open patio doors. Rain blew in. He slammed the doors shut.

The silence which followed was not romantic. It was downright miserable, punctuated only by the loud bursts of thunder and the luminous streaks of lightning. Suddenly he grinned and dragged a rueful hand through his thick black scrub.

'Do you really think I control the heavens?'

'Yes,' she hissed. 'And to think I've wasted my

time wishing upon stars!' With that she turned and fled into the bedroom locking the door behind her. She leaned against it, her breath coming in short tortured gasps as she strained her ears for any sound that he might still be in the penthouse. After several moments she thought she heard the front door bang and her heart fell to the pit of her stomach. Surely he hadn't gone? When she opened the door the penthouse stretched before her with an agonising emptiness.

The temperature had dropped dramatically with the advent of the storm, but Sarah didn't feel the cold as she wandered forlornly from room to room. She hadn't been totally responsible for what happened between them but she knew a large part of the blame rested with her. He had been struggling with his emotions and she had known this. She shouldn't have baited him. He had been teetering on the threshold of a new emotion, and she had foolishly pushed him to the wrong side of love.

Her restless wanderings brought her to Angus's bedroom. She stood in the open doorway for several seconds before entering. This was a man's room, with not even a hint of feminine intervention. The oak furniture was big and square, the lamps had dark marble bases, the shades were beige, the carpeting of the same colour with a chocolate-brown doona stretched across a massive king-sized bed. On the night-tables were several books on computers and the

latest in software electronics. Sarah ran her
fingertips lightly over these books, the night-
tables, the lamps and the doona. She reached
down and fluffed up the pillows, knowing his
head had rested on them.

He hadn't brought a change of clothing, and
when she opened the sliding cupboard doors saw
why. It was crowded with suits, sports jackets,
slacks and shirts. Another section revealed shoes,
two rows of them, dress shoes and sports shoes.
When she had put away her dress she had
wondered if it was possible to fill the massive
cupboard and the huge chest of drawers. Now,
looking at Angus's wardrobe, she knew it
certainly was!

The adjoining bathroom had the faint scent of
aftershave and talcum powder. It was all very
cosy, and she wondered what it would be like to
belong here truly as Mrs Angus Sawyer. Would
they divide their time between here and the
mansion on the banks of the Brisbane River, or
would the penthouse at Surfers Paradise be used
strictly as a holiday retreat? She caught her
reflection in the mirror and she couldn't help but
smile. She looked soft and dreamy, like a love-
struck heroine in a romantic movie.

Sarah sighed and looked at her watch. The storm
was still raging outside and she worried where
Angus could be. She shivered and rubbed her
bare arms with her hands, finally feeling the
chill. For the first time in her life she knew what

it was like to be cold both on the inside and the out. The fierce wind blew the rain across the tiled patio, soaking everything in its path. Visibility was almost nil. She drew the heavy curtains and switched on the lights which helped expel the gloom. She went into the kitchen and opened the refrigerator, then closed it again. She did the same to the oven and to the cupboards. It was something to do. Her restless wanderings took her into the library and she studied the titles of hundreds of books. She absently noticed that there wasn't a speck of dust to be seen anywhere. The penthouse, while beautiful and luxurious, suddenly seemed a cold, sterile prison.

'I've got to get out of here,' she announced to the empty walls. She stared at her watch. She had been taking readings every three minutes or so, but even so she was amazed to see it was almost four o'clock. At first her concern had been for Angus out in this raging storm. Her concern had gradually turned to guilt because she felt responsible for his going. Now she was filled with hurt that he had left her alone for so long without even ringing to explain his whereabouts or when he would be back.

Hurt gave way to anger that he should neglect her in such a fashion. Determined that she wouldn't be here when he returned, she wasted no time in leaving. She quickly discarded her shorts and top for the lemon-yellow dress she had planned to wear for dinner. She applied a light make-up and brushed her hair until it shone.

The storm was still raging outside but this didn't matter. She wasn't going far, not even outside. Angus had said the building housed several restaurants and she planned to dine in one of them. If he wasn't back by the time she returned then she would plan her next step. Right now she hoped he would come back, find her gone and worry himself sick about her, as she had done over him the whole afternoon.

She checked her handbag. Yes, she had enough money to keep her out for a while. Concern for her safety might be the catalyst the big lug needed to realise how much he loved her! A twinge of guilt pricked her conscience, but it wasn't enough to make her change her mind. Sometimes a girl's got to do what a girl's got to do, she told herself, and with this courageous thought she let herself out of the penthouse.

The bistro was crowded despite the early hour, and Sarah guessed that the tenants of the luxury units had decided it was far wiser to stay inside on such a treacherous evening than to seek other entertainment along the famous strip.

'A table for one, miss?'

Sarah looked at the maître d' and nodded. 'Yes, please,' she said looking past him into the crowded room. Everyone seemed to have somebody. There was a dance-floor and several couples were moving in time to a small but rather good band. She didn't notice the admiring glances she was receiving or how closely the maître d' was watching her hauntingly beautiful face, his own expression curious that such a beauty should be alone.

'This way please, miss.'

Sarah followed him to a tiny round table in a corner of the room. A small candle silently flickered in its glass globe. She stared down at it and its small light illuminated the tears in her eyes. It would be so easy to crush that tiny flame, to destroy it as simply as Angus had destroyed her heart.

The flame sputtered and dimmed and she held her breath, fearful that her thoughts would take away this friendly glow. She gently cupped the glass globe in her hands and drew it closer. The flame expanded and she allowed herself to become hypnotised by it, forcing Angus's image into the glow until it was him she held in her hands.

The handsome face appeared to smile up at her, jet-black eyes dancing with merriment and teeth a dazzling white against his darkened skin.

'Oh Angus,' she whispered. 'Where are you? How could you be so cruel as to invite me here and then leave me?'

A waiter appeared for her order and Sarah pushed the globe to the centre of the small round table, grateful for the darkened room which successfully hid her crimson cheeks. But if the waiter found anything unusual about a beautiful young lady whispering to a candle then he had the grace not to show it.

'White wine, please,' Sarah gave her order,

and when the young man left she stared again at the candle wondering how many broken hearts this particular one had seen. In a place like Surfers Paradise where people flocked from all over the world in search of adventure and romance there would have to have been the odd broken heart, a heart that felt just like hers!

The waiter returned with her drink and enquired whether she would be ordering dinner. The tables were set close together and Sarah saw that the occupants next to hers were eating lobster and salad.

'A lobster salad, please,'

The waiter jotted it down and shortly returned with her order.

'Would you like another drink, miss?' he enquired politely.

'Yes, another glass of white wine,' Sarah answered, and while she had no appetite for the delicious-looking food in front of her she knew she couldn't very well occupy the table without ordering something. Besides, the food and the wine would keep her busy. She glanced at her watch. She had only been gone an hour. She ate slowly, passing another hour before she asked for her bill. She left the bistro feeling weakened by her extravagance and by the food and wine which hadn't settled happily in her churning stomach.

Momentarily blinded by the bright fluorescent lighting in the foyer after the dim interior of the bistro, Sarah didn't see Angus and his stunning blonde female companion as they made

their way through the huge glass doors, laughing
as they shook rain from their shoulders. It was his
voice which she heard and immediately recog-
nised. No one had a voice quite like his with his
deep rich baritone and she would recognise that
laugh anywhere. It was the same laugh which
made her smile when she didn't want to, which
invited her to join in until her own laughter had
been as rich and as intoxicating as his own. Her
poor heart shuddered and crushed against her
ribs and she clutched her hand to her breast while
she fought for breath.

He didn't see her. He was too involved with
the blonde and the fact that she was wet to notice
the pale frozen figure dressed in a bright lemon-
yellow frock partially hidden by a huge potted
palm.

'Oh, that rain,' the blonde laughed as she
flicked back her dampened tresses before standing on her tiptoes to smooth back Angus's unruly
black crop. 'If we catch pneumonia over this I
shall hold you personally responsible.'

Angus laughed and draped his arm around her
shoulders. 'If we do, it will be worth it.' He
smiled down at the beautiful face turned up to
his. 'At least for me it will.'

'Are you sure you want me with you when you
tell Sarah?' the blonde asked anxiously. 'After
all, it was all your idea.'

'But I couldn't have managed without your
help. Besides I want her to hear everything.'

'Well, I would like to tidy up a bit before I

meet her. My hair's a mess and I think it's important that I make a good impression.'

Angus was in too good a mood to be annoyed by the delay. 'Women!' he laughed. 'All right, there's a ladies' room in the bistro. I'll wait for you here.'

Sarah could smell the blonde's perfume as she swept past her and into the bistro. Angus strolled to the far side of the foyer, his shoulders slightly hunched and his hands stuffed into his trouser pockets. He stood in front of an enormous mural and while he studied it Sarah slipped from her hiding-place and crept towards the lifts. She pressed the appropriate button and when the doors opened she darted inside like a small wounded animal.

Her pain was so acute that mercifully she didn't feel it. She was in a state of numbed shock. Only a remote part of her brain was functioning. It told her Angus had betrayed her and that she must escape. Escape before he and the blonde had the chance to tell her of their plans.

A pale ghost stepped from the lifts and entered the penthouse. This same ghost stuffed her clothing into her small case. The whole operation took barely a minute.

They weren't to know they passed each other in the lifts. While Angus was opening the penthouse door for the blonde to enter into his world of luxury, Sarah pushed open the lobby doors and raced blindly into the cold, wet, windy night.

Angus stood in the centre of the lounge. A sudden chill gripped his heart. Without warning he raced towards the patio doors and flung them open. The heavy curtains billowed behind him and the blonde stepped back from the incoming rain. His body stiffened and like a sleep walker he made his way to the guard-rail and leaned over.

There was a commotion on the street far below. Flashing red lights blinked up at him, but the only thing he saw was a small yellow object lying broken and twisted on the road. His agonising cry was worse than any thunder.

'*Sarah!*'

CHAPTER TEN

SARAH felt warm and cosy. She was in her own private world—a world where pain didn't exist. Nothing could hurt her here.

But someone was trying to drag her from her safe little cocoon. He kept calling a name, Sarah ... and she wondered if this was herself. Sometimes she felt a strong urge to respond to that persistent voice, but something held her back. If she awakened she knew she would feel that pain again, and the voice was somehow connected with the pain.

There were other voices too. There was the soft gentle voice of her mother, the gruff-sounding voice of her brother Billy and little Nellie's hesitant voice. She loved those voices, but they sounded sad and she wondered why this should be.

As she slipped in and out of consciousness the voices began to take shape. They had eyes and noses and ears and hair and they had hands which gently touched her and smoothed back her hair. The voices had lips which touched her cheek, but one—the one she was afraid of— sometimes touched her *mouth*!

At times these voices joined together and Sarah listened. She wondered why they sounded so fearful, or why they should be so worried. Didn't they know how safe and happy she felt in her snug little cocoon? She wished she could tell them not to be so sad, and sometimes she even dreamt that she had said this. But still they sat and waited, and she wondered whatever for.

But what was that new sound? It had been going on for a long time now and suddenly she no longer felt happy in her sheltered little world. Something was tearing at her heart and she felt the pain.

Now she was being lifted and she was going back and forth and she dreamt she was a baby and that Daddy was rocking her in the old farmhouse kitchen. The pain in her chest eased as she snuggled into the strong arms and oh, how safe and secure her world became once more.

'Sarah, oh Sarah. My own sweet little Sarah,' a voice above her moaned in such a pathetically ragged tone that Sarah had to listen.

Slowly she raised her thin limp arm to touch his cold wet cheek. 'Don't cry,' she begged. 'Please don't cry.'

'Sarah! Sarah! It's *me*, *Angus*.' He shook her. 'Wake up, Sarah, wake up. *Please!* Oh Sarah, Sarah, Sarah, please, it's *me*, Angus!'

Angus? she thought. Yes, she had once known a man named Angus and he had hurt her. She trembled and she didn't want to remember any more. If she remembered then she would start hurting again and she knew she couldn't stand that.

'Sarah, my darling, my own sweet love. I love you, I love you, oh, Sarah, please, *please!*'

But she already knew he loved her. She had known that even before he had, but he had been too afraid to tell her. Now she remembered all of it, and her trembles became violent shakings. He had been so afraid of his love for her that he'd found another woman—a blonde woman, tall and very beautiful, and they had been outside the lifts standing in the foyer and they were laughing and talking and planning how they were going to go upstairs to the penthouse to tell her of their love.

A faint smile touched her pale lips. But she had been too clever for them. She had run away. It was cold and wet and dark and she had raced across the street. Something had happened. Oh, yes, yes, now she remembered. Oh, the pain, the horrible pain and the lights! Red lights flashing in her eyes. Then the sweet nothingness when she hadn't felt anything, not anything at all.

'Sarah, Sarah, I'm not letting you go back! Stay with me, Sarah. Please, darling, you can do it. Do it for me. Do it for *us!*' he begged hoarsely.

'No!' she cried out. 'I don't want to!'

'Yes, you do! You do, Sarah. Hold on to me, hold on to me, that's it, that's my girl. Come back to me, Sarah. Come back, come back, come back . . .'

Her eyes opened, and to Angus it was the most beautiful sight he'd ever seen.

'Sarah,' he whispered, gently gathering her

closer in his arms. 'Oh, Sarah, my sweet little love.'

She stared up at the face only inches from hers, hardly recognising the bearded, gaunt figure holding her so tenderly in his arms. There was no seduction in these eyes, no mocking smile on the handsome mouth. She reached up and touched his cheek and she felt the dampness.

'Why are you crying?' she whispered. 'Have I done something wrong?'

The bloodshot eyes closed and he dropped his dark head to rest beside hers. She lay very still while his body shook with emotion. Her arms stretched around him and she nuzzled her cheek against his and the peace which came over her was far better than the one she had just left. And then she *remembered*!

Sarah sat up in bed and absently brushed her hair. She was thinking how much it had grown in the six weeks she had been in hospital. The first thing she would do when she was discharged tomorrow was to find a hairdresser and have it cut. She had lost so much weight that her wan little face seemed lost in the thick auburn mane. Her beautiful eyes were tortured pools of heartbreak and she felt cold and empty inside.

Her mother sat on a chair next to the bed and watched her daughter. Her expression was sad. 'You've always been a beautiful girl, Sarah,' she said quietly. 'Sometimes, when you were very little, I would look at you and think you had too much beauty, that it would get you into trouble somehow.'

Sarah put down her brush and smiled bleakly. 'Did you really think that?'

'Yes, but that was when you were little. As you grew up I began to realise it wasn't your beauty I needed to worry about. It was your stubbornness.'

Sarah closed her eyes. 'Mother, please. I know what you're leading up to and I don't want to discuss him.'

But her mother continued. 'You've changed, Sarah,' she said sadly. 'You were always one to see both sides of the coin, but now I look at you and . . .'

'Mother, *please*! There's nothing between Angus and myself. There never was. It was just wishful thinking on my part.' Her voice rose. 'He almost *killed* me! Don't you realise that? It's on account of him that I ran into the path of that car. You sit there and tell *me* you don't like what you see. That's because you're blinded to the facts just like I was blinded by my love for Angus. Instead of condemning me, you should be grateful that I woke up to myself before it was to late, before any more damage could be done.'

Her mother leaned forward and took Sarah's hand into her own. 'You mustn't blame Angus for what happened to you. He saved your life. He rarely left your side in all the weeks . . .'

Sarah snatched her hands away. 'I've heard a thousand times how dear wonderful Angus drew me out of my coma. Everyone thinks he's so damned wonderful,' she added bitterly.

'Well, he is!' her mother insisted staunchly. 'And you're a fool to deny it. The man *loves* you, Sarah!''

'If he loves me why hasn't he been around to see me for the past two weeks?'

'You know why he hasn't been here. Don't you think the man has feelings? You had him practically thrown from your room, insisting to your doctors and nurses that he shouldn't be allowed near your bedside. If you're ever to see that man again, Sarah Ames, you must make the first move.'

Sarah folded the hem of the sheet into neat little pleats. 'I'll never do that,' she said quietly. She looked up at her mother and there were tears in her eyes. 'I haven't told you what happened that night, Mom. I mean I . . . I told you some of it but not everything.'

Her mother got up from the chair and sat down on the edge of the bed and drew her daughter close. 'Tell me now, child,' she whispered softly. 'Tell me, then perhaps we'll both understand.'

Sarah's voice broke. 'I loved him so much. I think I fell in love with him the first day we met. Towards the end I thought he was starting to feel something for me too. In fact I was convinced of it. There had always been a sort of . . . magic . . . between us, and I thought that when we came to Surfers he was going to acknowledge that he loved me. Instead he . . . he left without even so much as a telephone call explaining his whereabouts, and then showed up at the penthouse with another woman. I . . . I . . . was in the foyer and I heard them talking. They were going to tell me about their plans for the future and . . .' Sarah covered her face with her hands and sobbed. 'I'll never forget how I felt. I felt like dying. I felt all crushed up inside.' She looked at her mother with tears streaming down her cheeks. 'And I never want to feel that way again!' she sobbed brokenly.

Her mother frowned. 'This conversation you said you heard. Are you quite sure you got it right?' She took some tissues and wiped Sarah's face. 'You were already upset. Perhaps you jumped to the wrong conclusion?'

'No! Angus *knew* he was falling in love with me and he was *terrified*. He wanted to get me out of his life and he almost *did*!'

Her mother shook her head and sighed. 'You'll never know unless you ask him. Please, Sarah, for both your sakes give him a chance to explain what happened that evening. You will never forgive yourself if you don't.'

'I'll never forgive myself if I *do*. He's had plenty of time to come up with any story he chooses. I can't understand you, Mother. I'm your *daughter*! Your loyalty should lie with me, not *him*! Surely you wouldn't want me to listen to any more of his lies?'

'Lies?' Her mother arched her brows. 'Angus

Sawyer is a man who does not lie.'

Sarah laughed—a broken sound. 'I can't believe this. No matter what I say you continue to defend him. The man is a rogue, Mother, a rogue! Would you want to see your daughter involved with a man like *that*?'

'You're not good enough for him!'

Sarah's eyes widened in astonishment. '*What?*'

Her mother stood up. 'You heard me. You've lost your spirit, Sarah. You're not strong enough for a man like Angus Sawyer. He deserves a woman with courage. A woman who would stand by him through thick or thin. He certainly doesn't need a woman who is filled with self-pity and self-righteousness. The man needs love, not scorn.'

Her mother's words stung and went straight to the core of her being. 'Don't worry about Angus, Mom,' she said in a small quivering voice. 'He'll never lack love. Everybody loves him. The trouble is . . . he never returns that love.'

Her mother stared thoughtfully down at her. 'Have you ever wondered why that should be?'

Sarah bowed her head. 'He told me once about his childhood. It wasn't very pleasant. He lost both his parents at an early age and he's been fending for himself since he was thirteen.' She turned her face away while fresh pain stabbed her heart.

'Did he love his parents?' her mother asked quietly.

Sarah nodded. 'Yes.'

'It's a pity then that the first time he loved and trusted again was wasted on you.'

'*Mother!*' Sarah gasped.

Her mother nodded. 'Yes, you have good reason to look so horrified. You have a lot to answer for, Sarah Ames.'

Sarah was discharged from hospital the next day. She stood alone on the hospital steps, her small suitcase clutched in her hand while a cold wind whipped around her legs and lifted the hem of her skirt. Her mother, Billy and Nellie had returned to the farm out of necessity, and Sarah was to join them in a few weeks when her doctors had given her the all clear. In the meantime she was to stay at Surfers Paradise to continue physiotherapy.

She looked at the folded piece of paper in her hand. It was the address of a small flat her mother had found for her close by the hospital. She stepped down towards the taxi rank to wait in a short queue. Her pale green suit hung on her thin body like a shapeless bag. She didn't see Angus. Her head was bowed into the wind, and there were tears of despair in her sad green eyes.

'I have a car waiting for you, miss,' he said firmly, gripping her arm and leading her towards the red Maserati.

Taken by surprise, and in her weakened condition, Sarah didn't argue. Angus opened the door and helped her inside, his hands gentle as he fastened the seatbelt around her. He tossed her case into the back and slipped into the seat beside her.

Sarah lifted her hand to give him the crumpled piece of paper. 'This is where I'll be living for a while,' she said in a small voice. 'I ... haven't read the address.'

He took the scrap of paper and tossed it out of the window. 'You're in my hands now!' Without a further word he started the motor and drove to the penthouse.

It all seemed like a dream. Astonishing that the foyer still looked the same and, yes, there was the huge potted palm she had hidden behind. Over there were the lifts. Once inside she saw the glossy printed photo of the bistro where she had had her dinner and it seemed as if it had all happened a thousand years ago.

Angus unlocked the door to the suite and taking her arm, led her inside. She would only be here a few minutes. He had thrown away the address of the flat but it would be easy enough to find another close to the hospital. She wouldn't worry about that.

Her future belonged to only her now and she would plan it one step at a time. When she was stronger she would go somewhere and start all over again.

He led her to a chair and gently pressed her into it. She had almost forgotten how gentle he could be and she didn't want to be reminded. Her wounded heart was still very tender, and her scars not yet healed. She doubted she would ever get over him, but if she had any chance for the future it rested with her now. She wouldn't let him get to her. She wouldn't!

He dragged a chair close to hers and sat down in front of her, their knees almost touching. She raised her haunted eyes to his and took a deep breath, determined that whatever he said to excuse his actions that night would be listened to, but certainly not accepted.

And so she looked at him, really looked at him and she was horrified by what she saw. He had lost weight and his eyes seemed like two feverish black orbs burning in their hollow sockets. Her heart cried out to him, but she quickly silenced it. He had suffered too, but not as she had. He was ravaged by guilt for what he had done to her. He reached for her hands but she quickly moved them away. After all he had done did he still think he had the right to touch her? she wondered. But even so she winced when she saw pain flash in his eyes at her rejection.

'I know you hate me, Sarah,' he said in a ragged voice.

'No, I don't hate you, Angus,' she answered quickly.

Faint hope glimmered in his eyes. 'Well, at least that's a start.'

A cruel smile hardened her lips. 'You didn't let me finish, Angus,' she said softly. 'The reason I don't hate you is that I don't feel anything towards you at all. I neither like nor dislike you. As far as I'm concerned you don't exist.' She moved towards the edge of her chair and smiled coldly. 'I'm glad I've said that. I've been wanting to for a very long time.' She started to get up but he pushed her back, grabbing her hands and holding on to them despite her frantic attempts to free herself.

'There's something *I've* been wanting to say to *you* for a very long time!' He searched her coldly passive face. 'I love you, Sarah. I've always loved you! If you had died I would have too.'

She laughed at this absurd confession. 'You can't appease your conscience by saying you love me, Angus. I happen to know you better than you think.' She looked down at his hands holding hers. 'Let me go please. You're hurting me.' He released her hands and she smiled triumphantly. 'Thank you. That was the last time you will ever hurt me, Angus Sawyer.'

An agonised cry tore from his throat. He grabbed her from her chair and crushed her to his chest. 'I've never wanted to hurt you. You must believe that. I only want to love you, to show how *much* I love you. You've got to believe me, Sarah.' Suddenly he held her away and she felt him tremble. He cupped her cold little face in his hands, his thumbs gently caressing her pale cheeks.

'You are the most precious, the most wonderful thing that has ever happened to me and I can't, I just can't let you go,' he cried raggedly.

Sarah tried to steady herself. The wall she had painfully built around her heart was slowly starting to crumble. 'I waited so long to hear you say those words, Angus,' she said in a voice thick with unshed tears. 'I wanted your love more than anything in the whole world.'

'You've got my love, Sarah. You've *always* had it!'

She shook her head sadly. 'I believed once that you might love me, Angus, but I don't any more.' A shuddering sigh escaped her lips. 'Please don't feel guilty over what happened. The accident was my fault. I was reckless and careless. *Too blinded by tears to see where I was going!*'

'Tell me about that night,' he pleaded hoarsely. 'I've got to know.'

She stared at him. 'Surely you've worked that out for yourself.'

'No, I've tried! A thousand times I've tried. I traced your movements. I know where you had dinner, but not why you ran out on to the street.'

Sarah rose slowly to her feet while he held on to her hands. 'I got tired of waiting for you, Angus. Surely you remember how you left me alone that day? I thought you must have forgotten that you had brought me with you. Eventually I got hungry so I went downstairs to eat. I saw you with a blonde and I heard you talking.' She looked accusingly down at him. 'And *laughing!*'

He merely nodded. 'Yes, that was Linda Sharp. *Mrs* Linda Sharp. She and her husband work for me. I was in conference with them the whole afternoon. I was taking Linda up to meet you and her husband was to join us later.' He stared at her, genuinely puzzled. 'Is that why you ran? Because you saw me with Linda?'

'Why, yes,' Sarah whispered, her knees feeling weak. 'I . . . I thought you . . . you and she . . .'

He jumped to his feet and placed his hands on her shoulders. 'You thought she and I were *lovers*?' he asked incredulously.

'I didn't know what to think. I . . . I . . . oh yes, I did think that. What else was I to think? You were angry when you left me and . . . and when you didn't come back I . . .'

'Sarah, look at me,' he commanded and she slowly raised her eyes to his. 'Do you remember the social club we started at the plant for the young people? Remember we talked about it all that morning, and we discussed the hardships some of the kids were experiencing? Do you remember that, Sarah?' he asked urgently.

'I remember,' she whispered.

'Well, that's what I was doing while I was with Linda and Ted. I was finding out about scholarships and how to go about granting them. I love you Sarah; I wanted to do something special. I wanted to . . . to *honour* you!'

'To . . . to *honour* me?' she asked weakly. 'Your love would have done that, Angus.'

He smiled suddenly. That old wonderful smile that she loved so much. 'But you know what I'm like. I like to do things in a big way. Sit down. I want to show you something.'

Sarah sat down and watched him cross the room in his long easy stride. He pulled open a drawer and took out a very important-looking document. He came back and handed it to her. 'I thought I would never be given the chance to show you this,' he solemnly declared.

Sarah stared at the document in her hands and slowly read the words emblazoned upon the surface: THE SARAH SAWYER SCHOLARSHIP.

Tears blurred her vision. At last she understood. He had wanted to admit his love that day, just as she had thought, but the only way he could think of doing it was through the scholarship. He had placed her on a pedestal and made her immortal by naming the scholarship after her. He loved her more than she had ever dared dream but what was more important, he planned to love her for ever! A sob tore from her throat as he gathered her in his arms, and it was a long time before either was capable of speech. Then they both started talking at once.

'I'll make us a pot of tea,' Angus said, looking down at her so tenderly that she thought she saw his heart in his eyes.

'No, let me.' She put her arms around his neck and kissed him. 'I love you so, my darling, that it positively excites me to think of doing the slightest thing for you.'

He laughed, a rich warm sound. 'We'll make it together.'

Hand in hand they strolled into the kitchen to make their tea. They were like two happy school children left in a room filled with their favourite sweets. They talked and laughed and kissed and hugged and lots of what they said didn't make any sense at all, but who cared? They were listening to each other's hearts, not to mere words.

'I suppose we should get married,' Angus said after they had drained the teapot dry.

'Yes, I suppose we should,' she answered teasingly.

'Could it be done today, do you think?'

She laughed her delight. 'I suppose it could, but it wouldn't be fair to Mom and the kids. I wouldn't want them missing our wedding for the world.'

'You're right of course. You have a wonderful family and I'm glad I'll be a part of it.' He raised her hands and kissed each pink-tipped finger. 'You're very much like your mother, you know.'

'Do you think so? I'll have to tell her that. She'll be very surprised, especially after what she told me about myself yesterday in hospital.' With her hands still clasped in his she pulled them forward and began to kiss each of his fingertips. 'I'll tell you some day, but not now.'

Angus chuckled. 'Let's save it for our honeymnoon. We'll compare notes.'

Sarah's eyes danced with delight. 'Don't tell me she raked you over the coals as well?'

He nodded and grinned. 'She said we were

both so strong-willed and stubborn that we deserved each other.'

Sarah pretended to be indignant. 'Imagine a mother saying a thing like that about her very own daughter! Stubborn and strong-willed indeed!'

'Well, you are, you know.'

'Humph! Look who's talking. You're the one who took so long to decide you loved me!'

'And that's where you're wrong! I fell in love with you that day I interviewed you in my office. It was five minutes after I met you,' he said so seriously that she knew he spoke the truth. 'That's why I kept finding excuses to visit the plant. It was just to see you.'

She was astonished. 'Why didn't you let me know?'

'I tried but you always managed to block my every move. I thought you hated me!'

'It was your reputation,' she sighed. 'I was determined not to become just another one of Angus Sawyer's women.'

'And that was the biggest charade of all.' He smiled down at her. 'I know you believed I was Queensland's most eligible bachelor, but from the moment I laid eyes on you I lost interest in any other woman. I was yours whether you liked it or not!'

'Oh, Angus,' she sighed happily, snuggling into his arms. 'I'm so sorry you had to wait until today to learn I love you.'

His black eyes gleamed wickedly down at her.

'I didn't! While you were in a coma you kept telling me how you loved me.'

She leaned back. 'I didn't!' She peeped inquisitively up at him. 'Did I?'

'You did and lots more besides!'

Sarah was horrified. 'You mean I ... I confessed things?'

'Yup! You told me you'd loved me for months and that all the times you were mean to me it was because you were afraid to show it.'

'Angus, are you making this up?'

'Would I do such a thing?'

'Oh Angus, we've been such fools. Mother was right. We were stubborn, both of us.'

'No, it was more serious than that. We were both afraid of rejection.'

She stared at him. 'Rejection? Were you really afraid I might not love you?'

'Afraid? I was *terrified*!' He tenderly traced the line of her cheek. 'When I saw you lying on the road ...' His voice trailed away and he shuddered. 'My world came to a halt, and it didn't start again until you opened your eyes in hospital.'

She pressed her cheek against his. 'I knew you were there,' she whispered softly. 'I knew you were always there.'

'And I always will be,' he declared solemnly.

Their arms circled around each other and when the sun cast shadows across the room neither noticed.

'I love you, Sarah,' he said simply and her

breath caught in her throat at what she saw in his eyes. He began kissing her, kisses which swiftly turned to passion and she clung to him, feeling the power of his body, the urgency in every bone as finally their hearts beat as one.

Six weeks later Sarah and Angus took their wedding vows. Neither ever broke a single one!

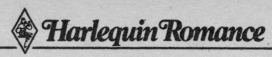
✦ Harlequin Romance

Coming Next Month

2869 CARPENTARIA MOON Kerry Allyne
Photographer Eden arrives to be tourist director at an Australian
cattle station, asked by Alick, a friend, but finds the station is
owned by his older brother who regards her as the latest girlfriend
Alick is trying to dump!

2870 WINNER TAKE ALL Kate Denton
When a campaign manager recommends that her boss, a Louisiana
congressman, find a wife to dispel his playboy reputation, she
never thinks she'll be the one tying the knot!

2871 FORCE FIELD Jane Donnelly
For a young amateur actress, playing Rosalind in an open-air
production in Cornwall is enjoyable. But being emotionally torn
between the estate owner's two sons, a sculptor and an artist, is
distressing—until real love, as usual, settles the matter.

2872 THE EAGLE AND THE SUN Dana James
Jewelry designer Cass Elliott expects to enjoy a working holiday
until her boss's son unexpectedly accompanies her and their arrival
in Mexico proves untimely. She's excited by the instant rapport
between herself and their Mexican host, then she learns that Miguel
is already engaged....

2873 SHADOW FALL Rowan Kirby
Brought together by a young girl needing strong emotional
support, a London schoolteacher and the pupil's widowed father
fall in love. Then she learns of her resemblance to his deceased wife
and can't help wondering if she's just a substitute.

2874 OFF WITH THE OLD LOVE Betty Neels
All of Rachel's troubles about being engaged to a TV producer
who doesn't understand her nursing job and expects her to drop
everything for his fashionable social life are confided to the
comfortable Dutch surgeon, Radmer. Then, surprisingly, she finds
Radmer is the man she loves!

Available in November wherever paperback books are sold, or
through Harlequin Reader Service.

In the U.S.
901 Fuhrmann Blvd.
P.O. Box 1397
Buffalo, N.Y. 14240-1397

In Canada
P.O. Box 603
Fort Erie, Ontario
L2A 5X3

**A chilling new mystery by
Andrew Neiderman**

ILLUSION

They were madly in love.
But suddenly he disappeared without a trace.
Confused and disappointed, she began to ask
questions . . .

Only to discover that her lover had actually been dead for
five years.

Available in SEPTEMBER at your favorite retail outlet or reserve your copy for August shipping by
sending your name, address, zip or postal code along with a check or money order for $4.70 (includes
75¢ for postage and handling) payable to Worldwide Library to:

In the U.S.

Worldwide Library
901 Fuhrmann Blvd.
Box 1325
Buffalo, NY 14269-1325

In Canada

Worldwide Library
P.O. Box 609
Fort Erie, Ontario
L2A 5X3

Please specify book title with your order.

 WORLDWIDE LIBRARY

ILL-1

ATTRACTIVE, SPACE SAVING BOOK RACK

Display your most prized novels on this handsome and sturdy book rack. The hand-rubbed walnut finish will blend into your library decor with quiet elegance, providing a practical organizer for your favorite hard-or soft-covered books.

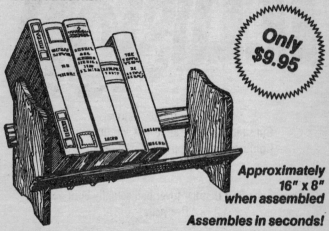

Only $9.95

Approximately 16" x 8" when assembled

Assembles in seconds!

To order, rush your name, address and zip code, along with a check or money order for $10.70* ($9.95 plus 75¢ postage and handling) payable to *Harlequin Reader Service*:

Harlequin Reader Service
Book Rack Offer
901 Fuhrmann Blvd.
P.O. Box 1396
Buffalo, NY 14269-1396

Offer not available in Canada.

BKR-1A

*New York and Iowa residents add appropriate sales tax.

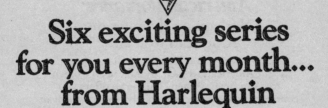

Six exciting series for you every month... from Harlequin

Harlequin Romance·
The series that started it all

Tender, captivating and heartwarming...
love stories that sweep you off to faraway places
and delight you with the magic of love.

♦

Harlequin Presents·
Powerful contemporary love stories...as individual as the women who read them

The No. 1 romance series...
exciting love stories for you, the woman of today...
a rare blend of passion and dramatic realism.

♦

Harlequin Superromance®
It's more than romance...
it's Harlequin Superromance

A sophisticated, contemporary romance-fiction
series, providing you with a longer,
more involving read...a richer mix of complex plots,
realism and adventure.

Harlequin
American Romance™
Harlequin celebrates the American woman...

...by offering you romance stories written about American women, by American women for American women. This series offers you contemporary romances uniquely North American in flavor and appeal.

◆

Harlequin Temptation
Passionate stories for today's woman

An exciting series of sensual, mature stories of love...dilemmas, choices, resolutions... all contemporary issues dealt with in a true-to-life fashion by some of your favorite authors.

◆

Harlequin Intrigue
Because romance can be quite an adventure

Harlequin Intrigue, an innovative series that blends the romance you expect... with the unexpected. Each story has an added element of intrigue that provides a new twist to the Harlequin tradition of romance excellence.

Harlequin Books®

PROD-A-2

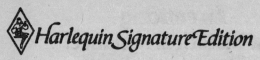

Penny Jordan

Stronger Than Yearning

He was the man of her dreams!

The same dark hair, the same mocking eyes; it was as if the Regency rake of the portrait, the seducer of Jenna's dream, had come to life. Jenna, believing the last of the Deverils dead, was determined to buy the great old Yorkshire Hall—to claim it for her daughter, Lucy, and put to rest some of the painful memories of Lucy's birth. She had no way of knowing that a direct descendant of the black sheep Deveril even existed—or that James Allingham and his own powerful yearnings would disrupt her plan entirely.

Penny Jordan's first Harlequin Signature Edition *Love's Choices* was an outstanding success. Penny Jordan has written more than 40 best-selling titles—more than 4 million copies sold.

Now, be sure to buy her latest bestseller, *Stronger Than Yearning*. Available wherever paperbacks are sold—in October.

An enticing
new historical romance!

Spring
Will Come

SHERRY DEBORDE

It was 1852, and the steamy South was in its last hours of
gentility. Camille Braxton Beaufort went searching for the
one man she knew she could trust, and under his protec-
tion had her first lesson in love....

Available in October at your favorite retail outlet, or reserve your copy for September shipping by sending your name, address, zip or postal code, along with a check or money order
for $4.70 (includes 75¢ postage and handling) payable to Worldwide Library to:

In the U.S.	In Canada
Worldwide Library	Worldwide Library
901 Fuhrmann Blvd.	P.O. Box 609
P.O. Box 1325	Fort Erie, Ontario
Buffalo, NY 14269-1325	L2A 5X3

Please specify book title with your order.

 WORLDWIDE LIBRARY

SPR-1